DEEP COVER

DEEP COVER

THE EXTRACTOR SERIES BOOK 4

MIKE RYAN

Cover Design by The Cover Collection

Edited By Anna Albo

1

Bridge and Nicole walked into the hotel lobby. Almost immediately, they saw Chris Abbott spring out of his chair and run toward them.

"Oh no, not again," Bridge said.

Bridge spun around to leave, but Nicole grabbed his arm and spun him back around again.

"What's with this turning around and trying to leave on people thing you got going on now?"

"It's not a thing," Bridge answered.

"Yes, it is. You did it last month too, on that model kidnapping case. You didn't want to talk to her either. It's like your thing now."

"It's not a thing."

"Sure seems like a thing."

"It's not."

"OK. But it seems like it is."

Bridge looked down at Nicole's hand, which was

still firmly grasping his arm. "Can you let go of me now?"

"Not till we do this."

"Don't do this to me."

"Just hear him out," Nicole said.

"Oh, Mr. Bridge!" Abbott yelled, putting his arm high in the air to make sure he was seen and heard. Not that it was easy to overlook him. Abbott was in his late twenties, but he was tall and thin and had a high-pitched voice. His voice was unmistakable, carrying through whatever room he was in.

Bridge closed his eyes and sighed. "Please. If you let me go now, I still have enough time to sneak out of here."

Nicole laughed. "Just listen to him."

"Nic, I've listened to him three times! My answer's not going to be any different this time than it was the last one."

"Well, maybe he'll have something different to say this time."

"Awe, come on, you know darn well he's not."

"We're in the business to help people. Not turn them away."

Bridge turned to look her in the eyes. "We're in the business to help people and take on cases that we can actually do something with. Not this."

"Well, he's already here. If you run away today, he'll just come back tomorrow."

"So I'll make up a different excuse. If you let me go, I'll give you sex as many times as you want later."

Nicole stared at him as if she was seriously thinking about it. "Just listen to him."

"You're passing up sex?!"

She shrugged. "I'll get it later anyway. You know you can't resist me."

Bridge sighed, knowing she was right. By the time Bridge took his eyes off his beautiful girlfriend, Abbott was almost standing in front of them.

Bridge huffed. "Awe, it's too late now. See what you did."

Nicole smiled. "Hi, Mr. Abbott, so nice to see you again."

"Oh, very nice to see you again too." Abbott shook her hand.

"It's been a while. Almost three or four days, I think."

"A week to be exact."

"That long, huh?" Bridge said.

"Could we go up to your room and talk?" Abbott asked.

Bridge sighed and looked at his girlfriend. "Sure." He put his hand out and flung it in the air in frustration. "Follow me."

The three of them got on the elevator and went up to Bridge's room. Bridge went into the kitchen and poured himself a drink.

"Won't you sit down?" Nicole pleasantly said to their guest.

"Yes, thank you," Abbott replied.

Bridge came back into the room, only half paying attention to Abbott as he sat down and checked his email on his phone.

Nicole looked at her boyfriend and shook her head. "Why don't you go ahead and start?"

Abbott cleared his throat. "OK, well, I'm sure you remember, I'm still looking for my brother's murderer."

"Chris, my heart goes out to you, it really does." Bridge put his phone down on his lap for a moment. "But I'm not a private investigator or a police officer. Just let them do their jobs."

"It's been a year since he was killed. They're giving up. Or have given up. Isn't that what happens after a while when a case isn't solved? They give up and it becomes a cold case?"

"Even if it does, I don't take those kinds of cases. I don't investigate murders. That's not my thing."

"Please, Mr. Bridge, I don't know who else to turn to."

"Call the police and ask to speak to the lead investigator."

"I've done that. They just keep telling me they have no leads."

"Then maybe there aren't any. I'm sorry to say this to you, but not every murderer gets caught. That's just life."

"I can't give up. Not yet."

"Listen, here's what you should do. Go home, look up a bunch of private investigators, and hire one. I'm sure they'd be glad to help."

"I can't."

"Why not?"

"I've already done that," Abbott said.

"You what?"

"I already hired one."

Bridge looked at his girlfriend with a confused look on his face. "Then what are you doing here?"

"Well, after our last meeting a week ago, you suggested the same thing."

"It was good advice."

"I took it and hired one the same day."

"See? Good for you. What are you doing here then?"

"Well, he went missing yesterday."

"Say what?"

"He started looking into my brother's death, and he went missing yesterday."

"How do you know he's missing?" Nicole asked. "Maybe he just hasn't checked in yet."

Abbott shook his head. "No. He's given me an update every morning since I hired him. Except yesterday. I didn't get one. Now, initially I thought maybe he was just busy, so I just figured I'd wait. But I haven't got one today either."

"Might still be busy," Bridge said.

"I don't think so. See, yesterday, well, maybe I didn't wait so patiently. Last night, I tried to call him. The phone rang six times, then went to voicemail."

"So?"

"This morning I tried to call him and the phone didn't ring. It just went straight to voicemail."

"Somebody turned it off," Nicole said.

Abbott nodded. "Yes."

"Might've been your PI that did it," Bridge said. "Like I said, he might be busy and into something and didn't want to blow off what he was doing."

"I don't think that's it. I think it's something more serious."

"Listen, if this guy is missing, you should call the police so they can start looking for him. Maybe call the FBI too."

"They won't help. I know they won't."

Bridge sighed and flicked his lips together, feeling like he wasn't getting through to him. "Listen, I'd like to help you. I really would. But we have another case coming up that's gonna take us out of the country."

"We do?" Nicole asked. The surprised tone of her voice should have given away that it was a lie.

"We do," Bridge replied sternly.

"I know you're not cheap, but I can afford to pay you extra," Abbott said.

"It's not about the money."

"Even if you could just look into it for a couple of days before you leave. I would really appreciate it."

"I just don't think we have enough—"

"We can look into it for a couple days," Nicole blurted out.

Bridge's eyes widened, and his face became a mixture of shock and anger as he stared down his girlfriend.

Nicole wasn't really concerned with his stare, though. She knew he'd get over it in a few minutes, and she wasn't worried about him falling in line. He always did after his initial objections. "We can give it three days."

A look of relief swept across Abbott's face. "Oh, thank you so much. I really appreciate it."

"You'll have to give us everything you know about your brother and the PI who was working on it. What he was doing, where he was going, people he knew, everything you can think of. It doesn't matter how small or insignificant you think it is. Write it down. We'll judge whether it matters or not."

Abbott smiled and nodded. "No problem."

Nicole went over to the kitchen counter and grabbed a legal pad and a pen, bringing them back to the living room and handing it to their guest. As Abbott began writing, Nicole sat down and leaned back, looking at Bridge, who was still staring her down. She tilted her head and plastered on a fake smile, trying to look as pretty and innocent as possible. Bridge squinted his eyes as he continued staring.

"Love you," Nicole mouthed silently.

Bridge put his thumb in the air and motioned for her to meet him in the bedroom. He then got up. "I have to check something," he said to Abbott.

Nicole waited a few seconds for him to disappear before she got up as well. "Would you excuse me for a second? You just keep on writing, OK? We'll be back in a second."

"Sure," Abbott replied. He was too focused on writing and his situation to really know or care what they were doing anyway.

Bridge was waiting in the bedroom with his arms crossed as Nicole came in. She closed the door behind her.

"What do you think you're doing?"

Nicole shrugged, playing the innocent card. "Just trying to help someone who needs it."

"Oh no, don't do that."

"Do what?" She batted her eyelashes at him.

"That! That. That right there. Don't play that I'm-so-innocent thing you do sometimes to pull yourself out of trouble."

"Am I in trouble?"

"You know you are. I specifically said we couldn't help with this case, and what do you do? Offer to help. You know damn well I didn't want to take on this case."

"What's the harm in looking at it for a few days? We don't have anything else scheduled. At best, we find something and can help him get closure. At worst, we find nothing, and maybe he'll finally accept that there's nothing else that can be done, and he'll move on. Then you won't have to deal with him again."

"That's not the point. The point is, you specifically went against what I said. You undermined me."

Nicole moved in closer to him with a sorrowful expression and threw her arms around him. She then playfully kissed his lips a few times. "I'm sorry."

"I know what you're doing. It's not gonna work."

She then started kissing his neck. "What am I doing?"

"You're trying to use your womanly ways to get me to calm down and come to your side."

She continued kissing him. "I would never do that."

"Uh huh."

They locked lips for the next few seconds, with Bridge finally beginning to lose the steam coming from his ears.

"If you really don't want to take the case, then fine. I mean, if you don't want to help someone who's hurting, who's in pain, who's looking for answers, then fine. Just go out and tell him we've changed our mind."

"Me?!"

Nicole continued kissing his lips. "Well, you're the one who's not interested."

As Nicole moved to other parts of his body, Bridge started thinking about it, though it was hard to concentrate. He knew this was Nicole's intention. She always did this to him to get what she wanted. He hated how he was an easy mark for her.

"You know, sometimes I really hate how our relationship has evolved."

Nicole kissed him some more, stopping for a second. "You want to go back to the way it used to be?"

"No. No. But it was easier to say no to you before."

Nicole grinned. "I'm sure it was." She then kissed both sides of his face. She knew she basically had won him over. Bridge sighed. "I'm sorry. Should I stop?"

"Huh? No, not that. That you can keep doing."

"Then what?" She kissed his lips again.

"Fine."

"Fine, what?"

"Fine, we'll take the case."

Nicole stopped kissing him for a second, then planted another big one on his lips. "Awe, thank you, sweety. Thank you for doing this for me."

"Did I have a choice?"

"Not really."

"I didn't think so."

She put her hand on the side of his face and kissed him again. "You won't regret it."

Bridge watched her walk out of the room. "Somehow, I think I already do."

2

Bridge and Nicole spent the next two days trying to find the private investigator that was working on Abbott's case. They weren't having much luck. They were trying to work backwards, going off the information that Abbott had told them, with the information that the investigator had told Abbott. The places the PI said he was going didn't pan out with any useful leads.

Now, the last place they had to look was the PI's house, which also served as his office. They were sitting outside the house for about an hour, making sure the coast was clear.

"Why are we doing this?" Nicole asked.

Bridge scoffed. "Because you let your bleeding heart get in the way and promised to look into it. That's why."

"I don't mean that. I mean here. Now. Why are we just sitting outside this guy's house? We know he's single and doesn't have any family. It's not like we're gonna run into someone."

"What if someone knocked him off and is also in there?"

"So you do think he met with foul play!"

Bridge put his hands up. "Now, now, just slow your roll there, Spanky. I didn't say that. I just said it could be. Didn't say it was."

"You gotta admit it's suspicious that a PI takes a case investigating a murder, then a week later goes missing himself."

"I don't have to admit anything."

"Well, at least we don't have to go far for this one."

"If I had to go far, I wouldn't have gone."

Nicole gave him a look, then shook her head. "I don't understand why you're so negative sometimes. It's like... you wanna help people... but you don't."

Bridge put his finger in the air as if he was making a correction. "No. I want to help people that I can really help. What's our motto? Helping people that others have given up on. Helping people that no one else can help. That's what we do. Investigating murders isn't it. That's something the police do, and they're very good at it, so why should we get in their way? If they haven't found something, maybe it's because there was nothing to be found."

"Or they overlooked something. As good as they are, we all know it happens."

"It doesn't happen as much as people think. If there was something to be found, they'd have found it."

"Well, maybe we'll get lucky."

"One more day and we move on," Bridge said.

"We don't even have anything else right now. Why are you in such a hurry to move on to something that isn't there?"

"Because I don't like to waste my time on things that have no payoff. There's nothing wrong with having some rest and relaxation between jobs." He then looked at his girlfriend, who hardly ever let a day go by without having a bedroom encounter, though it wasn't always in the bedroom. "Well, relaxation anyway."

The reference wasn't lost on Nicole, who raised an eyebrow at him. "Are you saying you don't get enough rest?"

"That's not what I'm saying."

"Are you saying that I enjoy sex too much?"

"That's not what I'm saying."

"Because if you are..."

"It's not what I'm saying."

"I'm sure there's plenty of other men—"

"Nicole, it's not what I'm saying. I love you. I love how you are. I love how you could want sex at the drop of a hat even if there were twenty guns pointed at you. I would never complain about it." Bridge then thought for a moment. "Well, maybe I would if there were actually twenty guns pointed at us, but you get what I'm saying."

Nicole grinned, then went back to reading some of the reports they had, none of which Bridge paid much attention to. "Did you read this on how Abbott's brother died?"

"Killed in an alley or something, wasn't he?"

"According to the police report, it looked like he was killed somewhere else and dumped there."

"So?"

"So that would mean it was probably premeditated."

"Not necessarily. Just means that wherever he was really killed, the person who did it didn't want his body found there."

"Did you see what he did for a living?"

"Traveling salesman or something, wasn't he? Sold encyclopedias or something."

Nicole put the papers down and gave her partner the kind of look she usually did when he said something so ridiculous. "Encyclopedias? Really?"

"What? Don't they do that anymore?"

"I don't think so."

As Bridge sat there staring at the PI's house, something else occurred to him. Something he really didn't want to think about. He hoped he was wrong. But anytime someone said they were an international traveling salesman, his mind immediately went to the agency. Traveling salesman. It was a cover that he used many times in his days at the CIA. He finally let out a loud sigh, drawing a look from his girlfriend.

"What was that for?"

"Nothing," Bridge replied.

"Don't give me that. I know your sighs."

"You know my sighs? Don't you have anything else to do with your time than analyze me sighing?"

"Oh, this coming from the person who counts how many times someone knocks on a door!"

Bridge let out a fake cough. "Well, um, you know, that's different."

"How?"

"Uh, it just is."

Nicole rolled her eyes. "Uh huh. So what are you sighing for?"

Bridge didn't want to think about—or talk about— anything that would lead him deeper into the rabbit hole. He was trying not to think too hard about this case. If he did, the more he analyzed it, the more he was afraid of what he might find. And he actually would get drawn into it.

"Spill. Now."

Bridge sighed again. "Fine. I was just thinking about him being a traveling salesman, him being killed somewhere else, his body being dumped in an alley; a lot of things are adding up."

"What are they equaling?"

"That maybe there's something deeper in play here."

"Such as?"

"Well, maybe it's my old CIA training, but a lot of it is starting to sound familiar."

"It's just coming to you now? You've had two days to think about it," Nicole said.

"I didn't want to think about it. I didn't want to add it up. I just wanted to let it go. But since we're here, since you're forcing this thing on me..."

"I'm not forcing anything on you."

"Well, now that I'm actually focusing on this thing... a lot is coming into focus."

"Want to sharpen the picture for me?"

"You have a traveling salesman..."

"We got that part."

"Will you let me finish?"

"Go ahead."

"We've got a traveling salesman, a murder, a body that was killed elsewhere and dumped, a murder that was so clean the police have no leads and have made no progress in a year."

"And?"

"Then we have a brother who won't give up, and a private investigator who starts looking into things, then the PI goes missing."

"So what's that tell you?"

"This wasn't some mugging or a fight over a girl or drugs or something stupid like that. This has all the makings of a professional hit."

"That's kind of a big leap to take there, don't you

think?"

"Police have no leads, right?"

"Right."

"If it was a spur-of-the-moment thing or wasn't planned, there would be some kind of evidence, right? There always is when it's spontaneous. People panic. They don't think straight. They make mistakes. There was none of that with Abbott, right?"

"Clean in all aspects, so it seems."

"So who else makes clean kills?" Bridge asked.

Nicole cleared her throat, thinking of the possibilities. "Uh, well, could be the mob or some other criminal element."

"Or it could be some kind of government body that uses traveling salesmen as cover identities."

"You're saying the CIA killed this guy on our own soil?"

Bridge shrugged. "I'm saying maybe they're somehow involved."

"You blow my mind, you really do. I mean, among other things. But how you go from not wanting anything to do with this case, to going right to the CIA having this guy killed is amazing. I mean, some people just dip their toe in the water to see if it's warm first, but not you, no, you just dive right in."

"My mind works differently than others."

"You can say that again."

"That's part of what makes me special."

"I won't argue there."

"You also know I might be right."

Now Nicole did the sighing. "Maybe. There's a big chunk of stuff missing that we need to fill in before we can make that conclusion, I think. Like where the PI is."

"That's another thing. If this guy's missing, we both know why that probably is."

Nicole's voice became sad. "It's because he's probably dead."

"Right. There's no other reason he'd be missing for three days."

"Unless he's hurt and in the hospital or something."

"And he just happens to be in a coma?"

"Something like that."

"Or maybe some other case he was working on, like ten years ago, someone decided to come after him now, coincidentally, the same time he was starting to work on this thing?"

"A lot of coincidences here, huh?"

"Too many. I thought you didn't want to work on this thing."

"I don't."

"Seems like you're getting into it," Nicole said.

Bridge took a deep breath, then looked at his girlfriend. It was one of those looks he gave when he was being sucked into something that he didn't want to do but just couldn't help himself. He glanced back at the house, then leaned over closer to the window. Judging from his body language, Nicole could tell that something caught his eye.

"What is it?"

"I just saw a light in there," Bridge answered.

Nicole immediately looked toward the house. It was just as dark as it had been. "You sure?"

"Positive. It only flashed for a second or two."

"Maybe it was a car driving by or something. The headlight went through the window."

Bridge shook his head. "No. This was inside." He looked over at the folder that was still sitting on Nicole's lap. "This guy had no family?"

Nicole opened the folder and started reading it again. "No wife or kids. Parents are alive. He was an only child."

"Maybe it's the parents sneaking in." He then glanced at Nicole with a look of disbelief. She gave him the same face.

"You really believe that?"

"Uh, well, I didn't say I believed it. Just said maybe it was."

"Pretty sure if his parents were dropping by, they'd know where a light switch was."

"Probably."

"So what do you wanna do?"

"I don't want to do anything."

"What do you feel you should do?"

Bridge sighed. "I feel like we should go over to that

house and see who's sneaking around and if it ties in to Gary Abbott's murder."

Nicole smiled. "I thought that'd be your answer."

They got out of the car and headed over to the house. It was a modest house, two floors, with a single garage attached to the side of the vinyl exterior. There were two bedrooms upstairs and one downstairs, which Darren Bevell converted to an office for his PI work. As they approached the house, Nicole wondered what the plan was. If Bridge had one, he hadn't shared it yet.

"Do you have a plan for this?"

"Nope," Bridge replied.

"Oh. Good. How we getting in?"

"Probably the same way the other guy did. Through the back."

"Makes sense. I guess he's not just gonna waltz out the front door."

"Unlikely."

"How we gonna take him?"

"Whatever way possible," Bridge said.

They made their way around the house and stopped once they reached the back door. Bridge put his hand on the knob and slowly pushed it open. He snapped his head around to look at Nicole.

"It's not locked," he whispered.

Nicole whispered back. "Well, if someone's in there, did you really think it would be?"

Bridge gave her a face, then pushed the door open

more as the two of them went inside. They walked through the darkened house, not using their flashlights or flicking on any lights, since it would give their presence away to whoever else was in the house. After coming in through the back, they found themselves in an enclosed patio, which then led into the kitchen area. Thinking he heard something, Bridge put his hand out to prevent Nicole from going any further. He tapped his ear to signal her to listen. The noise was faint, but it sounded as if papers were being rooted through or being thrown about a room. Bridge then pointed in the direction he thought it was coming from. It was the downstairs office.

They moved in that direction, making sure they made no sound. Once they got near the office, they stood outside the door, listening to what was going on. Someone was definitely rooting around. And it sounded quite messy.

Bridge and Nicole started communicating with their hands, though it was an animated conversation. It was quite the hand argument. Bridge initially wanted to go in alone and have Nicole wait where she was, but she wanted them both to go in together. After arguing with their hands for a minute, she finally relented and gave in, even though she thought it was a mistake.

With their plans settled, Bridge took a deep breath, then quickly snuck inside the room, putting his hand on the wall to feel for the light switch. He finally found it and flipped it on. A man clad in black attire, including a ski mask, suddenly turned around from the corner of the room, where he was rifling through the file cabinet.

"Whatcha doing?" Bridge asked, a smug look on his face for interrupting the burglar's plans. He then looked at the rest of the room. "Look at this. Was this really necessary? You made a mess of it."

The masked man stepped away from the cabinet and toward the center of the room. He then pulled out a gun and pointed it at Bridge, who immediately did the same. They stood there, guns pointed at each other in a standoff.

"Get out of my way," the man said.

"Can't do that," Bridge replied.

"I'll kill you if I have to."

Nicole then appeared in the frame of the door, getting down on one knee to change the angle that the masked man had to shoot on. It would have been difficult for him to take out both people before they opened up on him.

"Don't think you will," Nicole said.

"What are you doing here?" Bridge asked.

"Probably the same thing you are," the man answered.

"Who are you?"

The man tilted his head. "That's on a need-to-know basis."

"What happened to Darren Bevell?"

"Did something happen to him?"

"Is he dead?" Bridge asked.

"Why don't you ask him?"

"I feel like we have a gap here."

"Step aside and let me pass and no one has to get hurt."

"Right now, the only one getting hurt is you."

The man shook his head. "I can take you out right now."

Bridge shrugged. "Maybe so. But if you do that, you're not leaving here either. Because she's an excellent shot, and she'll kill you before you can do the same to her."

"I'm OK with that. Because I'm not being taken, I'm not answering questions, and I'm not getting stuck here."

"So what do you propose then?"

"I told you. You let me pass or me and you won't see another sunrise."

"You're willing to go down for whatever this is?"

"Yes."

"Interesting."

"So what's it gonna be?"

Bridge took his hand off his gun and motioned toward the door. The masked man slowly started walking in that direction.

"Give me space," the man said, not liking how the two of them were crowding the door.

Bridge took a few steps back, while Nicole got to

her feet and also moved back a little. As the man got near the door, he gave a final look to Bridge.

"Maybe next time."

"There won't be a next time," Bridge said.

He suddenly lunged at the man, grabbing a hold of his neck. The two started wrestling around, eventually dropping to the floor as Bridge pulled down his opponent with him. They gave each other a couple of punches, neither of which had any mustard behind it and were easily shrugged off by both of them. After a minute of rolling around on the ground, they got back to their feet, where they started exchanging shots. Bridge got in a couple, then the man got in a few of his own. Bridge was actually stunned for a moment and dropped to one knee as he clutched his stomach. The man moved in to continue his assault, but Nicole spun the man around and started delivering a few shots of her own. She used her background in jiu jitsu to kick him a few times and keep him off-balance. At one point, though, he grabbed her leg and gave her a powerful right hand that landed flush on the side of her face, knocking her down.

Bridge regained his energy and rejoined the fight, with both men getting in an equal number of shots. After several minutes, the man finally got the upper hand on Bridge, picking him up and slamming him down on a small wooden table by the door. As he picked Bridge up, Bridge put his hand on the man's head and pulled the mask off of his face. Bridge then went crashing through the table, breaking it apart into pieces. The man quickly looked around for his gun, though he didn't initially see where it went. And he wasn't staying around to look for it. Nicole looked up and saw the man's blond hair. It wasn't a military or government cut, but it wasn't long either. She only got a short glimpse of his face before he sprinted out of the house as Bridge and Nicole lay there in pain.

Nicole was the first one back to her feet, though it felt like someone had taken a hammer to her face. She put her finger on her left cheek, though it hurt to touch it. She then looked down at Bridge, who was moving, but barely. It felt like he'd just been in a three-round MMA fight and got dominated the entire match. Nicole rushed down by his side, holding the back of his head.

"Are you OK?"

Bridge let out a moan. "I think this is what it feels like."

"What?"

"To be run over by a truck."

"You didn't get run over by a truck."

"Could've fooled me."

"You did get your ass beat though."

"Well, I didn't notice you doing your MMA thing over there either."

Bridge started moving around a little more and Nicole tried helping him back to his feet.

"Can you make it?"

Bridge held the small of his back. "I think my back's broken."

Nicole looked down at what was left of the table. "You sure put that thing out of commission."

"Are you sure I'm not dead?"

"Pretty sure."

"'Cause it feels like every bone in my body is broken."

"You always were a little dramatic."

"I'd like to see you get thrown through a table and see how you react."

"I'll pass. I'll live vicariously through you on this one."

After a minute had passed, though he was still sore, Bridge started moving his arms around and tried to stretch out his back. Nicole rubbed his shoulders.

"Looks like someone's gonna need something to relax them later."

"I don't think my body could take your version of relaxing," Bridge said.

"I promise to be gentle."

"Remember what you told me about not regretting taking this job?"

"Yeah?"

"Well, it's official."

"What is?"

"I definitely now regret it."

3

Bridge and Nicole walked around the office for a few seconds before he hunched over and put his hands on his back. Nicole grabbed hold of him and walked him over to a chair in the corner of the room.

"Here. Just sit tight for a few minutes."

Bridge opened and closed his eyes slowly a few times, hoping that would magically transform the pain and take it out of his system. It didn't work. "Do I look as bad as I feel?"

Nicole looked at him and nodded. "Well... I've seen you look better."

"I think I hurt so much that I can't even tell if that was a dirty comment or not."

Nicole laughed. "It was kind of in the middle."

"Oh."

"You just sit there for a few minutes. I'll start looking around."

"We may not have much time."

Nicole started looking through the desk. "Well, I doubt that guy's calling the police."

"What if he has friends?"

"Then we probably would have seen them by now?"

"He was looking through the file cabinet."

Nicole glanced around. "Looks like he checked everywhere. Wonder what he was looking for?"

"Has to be something that Bevell was working on."

"But if he had more than one case going, then it could have been anything. Doesn't necessarily tie in with our thing."

"Too many coincidences here, Nic. You know I don't believe in them. Everything with this guy just so happens to take place after he takes on the Abbott case. It's too much to believe it's got anything to do with anything else."

Nicole started going through some papers. "I don't even know what I should be looking for."

Bridge was able to drag himself out of the chair, though he still wasn't feeling too good. But he couldn't just sit there and let Nicole do all the work. Especially since they didn't belong there.

"You all right?"

Bridge tried to stand up straighter to stretch his back out. "I'll survive."

Since Nicole was checking out the desk, Bridge

figured he'd try his luck in the filing cabinet. After a few minutes, Nicole sighed.

"What's wrong?"

"It just..." Nicole sighed again. "I just... I don't know what's important and what's not. There are names and dates and places and... and I don't know what any of it pertains to. Considering we're on the clock here and can't stay here all night, I'd say this is probably a worthless endeavor."

Bridge glanced at his girlfriend and winced as a shot of pain went up his spine. He then looked around the room and saw a backpack on the floor. He then went over to it and picked it up.

"You know what, let's start shoving everything in here, and we can look at it later."

"That's a good idea," Nicole said. "Then we can take our time with it."

Bridge started to lean over to pick up some papers on the floor, but made a groan. Bending over was a problem for him at the moment. Nicole came over to prevent him from hurting himself more.

"Here, I'll get this stuff. You go over to the cabinet and start taking stuff out of there. That way you can stand up."

As Bridge walked back over to the cabinet, he saw another backpack nestled in between the file cabinet and a table that was next to it. He gingerly bent over and picked it up to start shoving papers and folders from the file cabinet inside it. Within a few minutes, they had every piece of paper and file folder that was in the room inside a backpack.

"Ready?" Nicole asked.

"Pfft. Am I ready? I've never been readier."

Nicole smiled. She took her backpack and put it on her shoulder, then she took the backpack from Bridge and slung it over the other shoulder. "You need me to put you on my back, too?"

"Is that another dirty comment?"

Nicole laughed. "Could be."

They started to walk out of the house, with Bridge feeling a little better. At least he didn't need help walking. As they got to the kitchen, they stopped upon seeing a bright light. It was coming from the back of the house where they came in. Nicole looked at Bridge to see what he wanted to do. He wanted to split up and pointed for her to go behind the kitchen table, while he went back to the living room, ducking behind the corner of the wall.

After a few more seconds, the light got a little brighter. It was obviously a flashlight that was coming toward them. Bridge and Nicole waited silently and out of sight, until the man, or men, got closer. Then they'd spring a surprise on them. They patiently waited until the person came into view. It was only one man. It could've been the same person they'd run into before for all they knew. Maybe he wanted a rematch. The man, in dark attire, passed through the kitchen. It looked like he was on the way to the office as well. He seemed to know the way.

As the man passed the corner of the wall that led into the living room, Bridge jumped out and grabbed him by the neck and shoulders and wrestled him to the ground. The man tried to put up a fight, though grappling wasn't really his specialty. Bridge easily got the upper hand and wound up sitting on top of the man, straddling his waist. Bridge reached his arm back and was about to deliver a knockout-type blow, but then heard the man beg for him to let up.

"No! Please!"

It was a familiar voice. An unmistakable one. One that Bridge could never mistake for anyone else. It was one that Nicole had heard from the kitchen as well. She ran over to the light and turned it on. With his vision clear, Bridge looked down at Abbott's face and relaxed his arm. He got off him and helped him to his feet. Abbott put his hand on his heart to signify his discomfort with the whole situation.

"You wanna tell me what you're doing here?" Bridge asked.

Abbott cleared his throat. "Well, um, I came here because, well, you know, Bevell's been missing, and I wanted to try to find a few clues."

"Isn't that what you hired us for?"

"Well, I wasn't sure if you were doing other things and..."

"You know this is breaking and entering, right?"

"Um, well..."

"You could be arrested for this."

"Wait, isn't that what you're doing here?"

"Not the same thing," Bridge replied. "We're professionals. We do this for a living. We're trained to take risks. We know how to do these things properly. You don't."

Abbott scrunched his eyebrows together, looking at some of the bumps and bruises on Bridge's face. As Nicole came closer, he noticed the same on hers.

"Why do you guys look like that?"

"That's another reason why you don't do things like this," Bridge said. "You never know who you'll run into. We ran into a friend who was here before us."

"Who was he?"

"Damned if I know."

"Looks like he worked you over."

"You don't say."

"We should go," Nicole said, still mindful of any other visitors.

"What exactly were you hoping to find?" Bridge asked.

"Honestly, I'm not sure. I was hoping to find something that would jump out at me."

"Well, you accomplished that one."

"Other than you, I mean."

"You're lucky you didn't get here twenty minutes ago and find that other guy before we did. Otherwise you'd be joining your brother right now."

"I just didn't think it would be a problem."

"Leave the investigative work to us. That's what you're paying us for, right?"

"Right."

"We should go," Nicole said.

Bridge looked back at her and nodded. He put his hand on Abbott's shoulder. "C'mon. We need to get out of here."

"Did you get a chance to search?" Abbott asked.

Nicole held up the two backpacks. "We sometimes take our work home with us."

"Oh." They began walking through the back of the house again. "Did you find anything yet?"

"Other than a big guy with a big fist?" Bridge replied. "No. But we've got a lot of stuff to sort through. So we're gonna do that while you go home and stay out of it. Right?"

Abbott sighed. "I guess so."

"Chris?"

"Fine. I'll go home and wait for you to call me."

"Much better."

They walked out of the house without any further incident. Still on the lookout for any signs of trouble, they walked around the side of the house and down the street back to their cars. Abbott was parked in the opposite direction. About halfway to his car, Bridge's eyes happened to look further down the street. It must have been a flickering light that caught his attention. He only saw it for half a second. Maybe it was the light from a cigarette being lit. Maybe it was the light from a phone being turned on. Maybe it was something else entirely. But he saw it.

Bridge knew where the light had come from, and there was a car parked there, but it was too dark to see any of the occupants. He kept his head looking straight ahead so whoever was in the car didn't know he was on to them. He nudged Nicole in the arm.

"There's a car up ahead. About thirty yards away. Don't make any sudden movements."

"Who you think it is?" Nicole asked.

"Don't know. Could be anybody, I suppose."

"You don't think cops would be watching the house, do you?"

"Tough to say. Maybe it's our friend from earlier. Just stay sharp."

They walked a little further, almost to Abbott's vehicle, when Bridge noticed the car make a sharp and sudden turn out of its parking space. The car roared ahead toward them, speeding up to get closer to them.

"Get down!" Bridge yelled.

He pushed Abbott over, using his own car as cover, while also getting behind it. Nicole dove to the ground as well. Just as they hit the pavement, bullets ripped through the air from an automatic rifle. It was a tense few seconds as Abbott's car became riddled with bullet holes. Glass from the windows shattered. Then the other car sped off into the night. Bridge peeked his head around the front wheel of Abbott's car to make sure no one else was there, even though he heard the tires squealing as it left the scene. He then poked his head above the hood, making sure there wasn't a second car in the area that was supposed to finish the job. Seeing nothing that looked like a threat, he turned back around to make sure the others were OK.

Bridge noticed a bunch of glass on top of Nicole. "You OK?"

She gingerly got up, brushing the small pieces of glass off her body. "Yeah. I'm good."

Bridge then looked to Abbott. "How 'bout you?"

Abbott sat up. "I think I'm fine." He then looked at his car and sighed. "Look at my car. Why'd they have to do that?"

"You're lucky the car's the only thing that's got holes in it."

Bridge glanced back to his girlfriend, who looked troubled. She was just staring out into the darkness.

"What is it?"

"Just seems convenient," Nicole said.

"How's that?"

"They would've had a better, unobstructed view of us if they did it sooner. They had plenty of time. But they waited until we were almost at the car."

"Like they wanted us to take cover."

Nicole nodded. "I'm not sure they wanted to kill us. Seemed more like a message to me."

"What kind of message?" Abbott asked.

"The kind that suggests we might be stepping on some wrong toes," Bridge answered.

"This was a warning," Nicole said.

"Who would do that?" Abbott asked.

"People who are very dangerous," Bridge replied.

"What's it all mean?"

"It means someone doesn't want us looking into this."

"Again, who would do that?"

"Someone who's got connections."

"So what are we gonna do?"

"You're gonna go home and get your car fixed."

"And you?"

"I'm gonna keep looking into it."

"Even after this?"

"I don't scare easily," Bridge said. "When people want me to do something, I generally tend to do the opposite. I don't like being threatened. And I don't respond well to scare tactics. If someone wants a fight with me... then they're gonna get one."

4

Bridge and Nicole spent most of the next day holed up in their hotel room. They had papers sprawled all over the place. On the kitchen table, on the floor, on the couches, the living room table, everywhere. They were putting papers into different piles, things they might need to look at further, things that piqued their interest, things that seemed like they had no bearing on anything, and plenty of things that they weren't sure about either way.

Bridge got up from the table to take a break, walking to the refrigerator to get a drink. He moved his arm and shoulder around, still feeling the effects from the previous night's encounter with the man dressed in black.

"My back's still killing me. I don't know how those wrestlers do it."

"What's that?"

"They get thrown through tables and chairs and off the mat a million times, and they keep coming back for more day after day."

"Well, they're trained in that sort of thing."

"Yeah, I guess." Bridge let out a small groan as he stretched his back. "Hope I don't run into that guy again anytime soon."

"Why? Don't think you can take him?"

"I can take him."

"Your face says otherwise."

"Yeah, well, maybe next time I'll shoot first and kick his ass afterwards."

"That's cheating."

"All's fair in love and war, right?" Bridge leaned up against the counter and made a few more moans and groans.

"Something wrong?"

"No. It's just that we've been looking at this stuff for four hours straight and haven't found anything yet."

"Anything conclusive. There's plenty that might have some meaning. We just don't know if it does yet. There's obviously something here somewhere."

"What makes you think that?"

"If there wasn't, why else would that other guy have been there? He must've known there was something that would incriminate somebody."

"Maybe he just thought there was. Or making sure there wasn't. He might not have known for sure either."

"Considering the bullets that came flying afterwards, I tend to think there's something here."

After consuming his soda, Bridge went back to the table and started sorting through documents and case files. Another hour went by before they finally found something. As soon as Bridge saw the address, something clicked in his mind. He held the paper out in front of him and stared at it for a solid two minutes. Nicole eventually noticed that he hadn't moved in a while.

"What is it?" Bridge was so focused on what was on the paper that he didn't even hear her voice. She finally put her hand on his forearm to break his concentration. "Luke?"

Feeling her touch finally snapped him from his stare. "Huh?"

"What is it?"

Bridge glanced at her and handed over the paper. Looking at him strangely, she took the paper and read it. It immediately rang a few bells for her too, but not in the same way as her boyfriend.

"You know what this is?"

"Yes," Bridge answered.

"I can't place it. But it looks... familiar for some reason. Like I've..."

"Been there before?"

"Or have seen it somewhere before," Nicole said.

"Probably because you have."

"What is it?"

"It's a CIA station here in New York."

"That's where I've seen it. I remember sending a few reports to this address before."

"I've been there," Bridge said. "I used to get missions from there, debriefings after assignments, things like that."

"But you worked out of..."

"Well, that was before then. Before I met you. But this was one of my first assignments... working out of there."

"How would Bevell get this address? Why would he have it?"

"That's the million-dollar question."

"The CIA somehow ties into this?"

Bridge stared at her. "Certainly looks like it's heading that way."

"But how?"

"Unless Abbott was an agent. Either for us or for someone else."

Nicole raised her eyebrows and nodded. "And if someone found that out, or someone who's connected to the agency..."

"They didn't want anyone digging further into Gary Abbott's murder and took him out too. Tie off loose ends."

"How far is this gonna go? And how far are we gonna take it?"

"As far as the clues lead us."

Nicole made a face like she wasn't especially

pleased to follow him in that direction. "I dunno, Luke. I mean, we left the CIA on great terms; they've given us no issues when we left or since then. I really don't want to make enemies with them if this is somehow tied directly to them."

"Who's the one who continuously tells me to help the people that need help? Even if it doesn't exactly coincide with our mission statement."

"Now you're gonna use my own words against me?"

Bridge laughed. "You've used them against me long enough."

"They can make things difficult for us if we don't do this right."

"I think we've built up enough goodwill over the years helping to do some of their dirty work that it shouldn't blow up over this."

"Depending on what we uncover."

Bridge sighed. "Yeah."

They looked through some other papers, though none of them ever got to the level of interest as the one with the CIA address. Bridge eventually went back to it, holding it in front of him as he stared at it.

"You know, staring at it isn't going to suddenly bring you an answer," Nicole said.

"It might."

"We need to find something else that ties this together."

As Bridge stared at the address, he thought of another way to get the answers they needed. And a lot faster than what they were doing now. He finally put the paper down and looked at Nicole.

"Or we can just speed things up."

"How do you plan to do that?" Nicole asked.

Bridge tapped on the paper with his index finger. "Talk with the man that runs this."

Nicole leaned back, surprised to hear him say it. "I dunno, Luke."

"Is there ever a better way at getting to the heart of a matter than by going right to the top?"

"Even if they're involved, they're unlikely to tell you anything."

"If there's one thing I learned when I worked there, it's that it's not always about what they say. Sometimes it's about what they don't."

"It might put a target on you."

"After last night, I'd say the target's already been painted on my back."

Nicole wiped her face. "You sure this is a good idea?"

"No." Bridge smiled. "But I think wherever this case is taking us... we'll get there a lot faster."

"I'm not sure I'm liking this."

"You're the one who begged me to take this case."

"Well, that was when I thought it was a simple murder. Besides, when do you ever listen to me?"

"I always listen to you. Especially when you start... doing things."

"Well, maybe you should start learning some willpower to resist me."

Bridge looked at her and smiled. "Impossible." He then leaned over and gave her a kiss. "I could never resist you."

"Except you did for a while."

"And you broke me down."

"Unhappy that I did?"

Bridge leaned over and kissed her again. "Never."

"I'm sorry I got us into this."

Bridge shrugged. "It is what it is. We both know that whenever we're on a case, we never know where it might lead, or who it might lead to. Just one of the perils of the business."

"You're sure you wanna do this?"

"No. But I think we have to."

Bridge got up and grabbed his cell phone. He dialed a number that he hadn't dialed in a long time.

"Hello?" a woman answered.

Bridge didn't miss a beat. "This is Alpha Two-One-Seven-Six-Five."

"What is your business?"

"I would like to speak with Pinnacle One." There was silence on the other end of the line. The operator wasn't used to someone asking for that. Bridge knew it was an unusual request, but that wasn't going to stop him from demanding it. "I need to talk to Pinnacle One. Today. You get him the message. Tell him it's about Gary Abbott. I can be reached on this number."

"I will see what I can do."

"Thanks."

Bridge hung up and looked at Nicole.

"How'd it go?"

Bridge shrugged. "We'll see. I put the line out. Now we just have to wait and see if we get a bite."

"No reason why we shouldn't. We left on good terms."

"You know as well as I do that leaving on good terms doesn't exactly mean you get a free access card to sensitive information should it ever come up."

"True."

Bridge went back to the table and started looking at more papers with Nicole, though he knew it was unlikely they were going to find anything else. He thought it was all going to hinge on getting the meeting he was requesting. About ten minutes passed before Bridge's phone rang. He looked at Nicole once it did, a little surprised he was getting a call so fast. He looked at the number. It was unfamiliar. He knew that meant it was probably the call he was hoping for.

"Yes?" Bridge said.

"State your ID," a man replied.

"Alpha Two-One-Seven-Six-Five." Bridge could tell by the voice that it was not Pinnacle One. He had a deeper voice than the one he was listening to. It was most likely one of his assistants.

"And your business?"

"I need to speak with Pinnacle One."

"What for?"

"It's about Gary Abbott."

"Who's that?"

"That's what I want to speak with Pinnacle One about."

"I'm not sure that's a good idea."

"Listen, you all know who I am and what I do. I'm on a case that I think has something to do with you guys. Now, you can either let me in on it so I don't step on any toes, or I can just go about it on my own and risk blowing something that you don't want blown. Now which do you prefer?"

It was quiet on the other end for about ten seconds. "Hold on."

As he waited, Bridge looked at Nicole and shrugged. He wasn't sure which way this was going yet. They might decide to do business with him, or they could decide to blow him off and hope he goes away.

After a good solid minute, the man got back on the phone. "Pinnacle One will see you in one hour."

"Where?"

"Bethesda Fountain in Central Park."

Before Bridge was able to get off another question, the line went dead. He looked at his phone for a second before putting it back in his pocket.

"Well?" Nicole asked.

"One hour. Central Park at the Bethesda Fountain."

"With Pinnacle One?"

Bridge nodded. "With Pinnacle One."

Nicole gave him a look. At least it was in a public place. That meant there would be no funny business. If it was in an abandoned building or somewhere with no people, that would give them pause to worry. But when meetings were done in public, there was usually little to fear in terms of one's personal health. Usually.

"What do you think?"

Bridge shrugged. "I really don't know. I really don't know."

"Well, at least the park is good."

Bridge nodded. "Looks like we're going for a stroll."

5

Bridge walked around the fountain until he got to the edge of the lake and watched a few of the rowers go by in their small boats. He touched his ear to make sure his earpiece was working.

"You on?"

"I'm here," Nicole answered. She was dressed in running attire, shorts, shoes, a baseball hat, all to try to disguise her appearance if their guests knew what she looked like.

"See anything yet?"

"Not yet."

Bridge looked at his watch. "Still got a few minutes."

Bridge took his eyes off the rowers and turned around. His eyes immediately went to the statue in front of him. The Bethesda Fountain was one of the largest fountains in New York, as well as in the world, standing over twenty-six feet high and ninety-six feet wide. It was also one of the more well-known fountains in the world. The sculpture in the middle of it, also known as Angel of the Waters, featured an eight-foot-high bronze statue. The angel carried a lily in one hand, while the other hand remained outstretched, to signify the delivering of a blessing from the water pouring down from around her feet and into the fountain.

Bridge walked around the fountain to stand in front of it. He looked around, and not seeing anyone, turned back around to look at the fountain again. It wasn't the first time he'd seen it. He'd been there many times. But it was always a peaceful feeling that came over him every time he was there. He sat down on the ledge of the fountain, his back to the angel as he waited for his visitor. Out of the corner of his eye he saw Nicole walking by, pretending like she was just a regular tourist. She then went up the steps that led up to the terrace, just off of Terrace Drive. She stood there and looked out, having a front-eye view of Bridge.

"Must be nice having an angel on your shoulder, huh?"

Bridge laughed. "If only that were true."

"Maybe you can figure out a way to keep her there."

"I think she'd be a little heavy lugging around all the time."

After only a minute or two, she looked to her right and saw several men dressed in expensive looking suits walk past. She knew who that was. A few of them walked down the steps on the way to meet Bridge, while a few more stood near her, just taking in the view and making sure that nothing happened to their boss. Not wanting to stay in such company, Nicole put her earbuds back in and started running, though she really went to a nearby path so she could get a better look at what was happening. She could still hear what was going on when Bridge was talking.

Bridge sat on the edge of the fountain, leaning forward, with his elbows on his knees, watching Pinnacle One's guards disperse as the boss moved closer to Bridge. Bridge didn't take his eyes off the sixty-year-old leader as he approached. Pinnacle One stopped just in front of Bridge, not looking at him, instead looking at the statue behind him.

"A beautiful sculpture, don't you think?"

"It is," Bridge replied.

Pinnacle One continued talking in his gruff-sounding voice. It was a deeper voice that had done a lot of barking out of orders over the years, though his tone had softened in recent times. "I must say it was a surprise to get a call from you."

"Was it?"

"It's been a long time since we've seen each other."

"Eight years isn't really that long."

"In this business... eight years is almost a lifetime."

"I guess it is."

Pinnacle One sat down next to Bridge. "So what's this all about?"

"Gary Abbott."

"Who?"

Bridge chuckled. "C'mon, don't play me for a fool. I worked for this agency a long time. I know how things work. I also know when things aren't what they seem."

"And you think you've got that here?"

"I do. Gary Abbott was an international salesman who died under mysterious circumstances a year ago."

"So? That happens to a lot of people."

"A man that had, on the surface, no enemies, killed somewhere else, then dumped in an alley. It was a super clean kill, police had no leads, and the case soon dropped off the map."

"Sounds like you're dealing with an intelligent killer."

"Or agency."

Pinnacle One smiled. "And you think that was us."

"Well, when a private investigator starts looking into the matter, then he suddenly disappears, it starts to sound off the alarm bells. Then when that investigator also has the address of a certain station based in New York, a lot of things start adding up."

Pinnacle One continued grinning. "Careful, Luke. Sometimes things don't always add up to what you think they will. Two plus two doesn't always equal four."

"Sure it does. It doesn't add up when you start

throwing in different equations to mask the true answer."

"You were a good agent. Too bad you're not still in the field."

"I'm good where I am."

"Yes, still making a difference from what I hear. That's always been in your blood."

"About Gary Abbott..."

"There's nothing I can really say about him."

"Sure there is. You just won't. I came here to give you the option of clueing me in on what's going on so I don't start stepping on toes that I don't want to step on. But if I'm kept out of the loop, I can't really help that much, can I?"

"You could always move on."

"Afraid I can't do that. I've been hired to do a job and I'm gonna do it."

"Regardless of where it may lead or whose path you may cross?"

"That's the way I operate. Always have."

"I know. That's what makes you unique. That's what makes you great. That's what makes you..." He started to laugh. "What is it you call yourself? The Extractor?" He kept laughing. "I must say I do enjoy that name. It's fitting, though. You earned it."

"Back to Gary Abbott."

"Why are you so hell-bent on believing that he's one of ours?"

"Are you saying he's not?"

"I'm not saying anything."

Bridge was tired of the games. He could see that he wasn't going to get anywhere this way. At least he could say he gave it a chance. He stood up, ready to leave.

"Well, you can't say I didn't give you a shot."

Just as he started to walk away, Pinnacle One grabbed his arm to prevent him from leaving. "Sit down." It was said in a warm fashion. He then nodded toward the ledge. "Please."

Bridge slowly sat back down, ready to hear whatever else the man had to say, though he still wasn't sure it would be much of anything. "Gary Abbott?"

"I am familiar with the name."

"He worked for you?"

"Not in the way that you think."

"He wasn't an agent?"

"No. But we did use him on a few things here and there."

"Why was he killed?"

"I don't know. That's something we've never been able to figure out."

"So it wasn't you guys that did it?"

Pinnacle One grinned. "Now, Luke, you know we don't operate on U.S. soil."

Bridge laughed. "Yeah."

"We did not kill him. But we did approach him two years ago about working for us."

"Why?"

Pinnacle One shrugged, not able to give away all

the details. "Well, let's just say he had a job travelling around the world, and we wanted to use that to the best of our abilities. He had a natural cover that we thought would blend in nicely with some of the things we were working on."

"What was he doing here when he was killed?"

"Nothing to my knowledge. At least nothing for us. Just one of those dumb luck type of things that got him killed."

"So you don't know who did it?"

"Oh, we briefly looked into it, making sure no one knew his connection to us. But we didn't find any leads to indicate who it was and nothing ever blew back to us. So the matter's been closed as far as we're concerned."

"And the fact that it was a nice, tight, clean job doesn't mean anything to you?"

"Like I said, just happened to be dumb luck."

Bridge took the paper out of his pocket with the CIA address on it. He held it up to show his former boss. "And the fact that a private investigator had this in his possession doesn't ring any bells for you?"

Pinnacle One took the paper from his hand and looked at it. "I can't honestly say for sure how this man would've come across this in his possession." He leaned over slightly. "You mind if I keep this? I would hate for it to somehow fall into the hands of someone less scrupulous than yourself."

"Go ahead."

Pinnacle One folded it and put it in his pocket. "Thank you."

"So what do you think happened to this PI who was investigating Abbott's death?"

"Can't say I know anything about it."

"You didn't have him taken care of?"

"I don't even know who he is."

"Darren Bevell."

"Doesn't ring any bells."

Bridge smiled. "You also said that before."

"Yes, well, I can say for sure that this man's name doesn't sound familiar at all."

"How 'bout the fact that I was shot at last night coming out of this man's home?"

"You were?"

"Yep."

"By who?"

"Well, I guess that's the sixty-four-thousand-dollar question, isn't it?"

"You don't believe it was us, do you?"

Bridge chuckled. "Well, it did cross my mind. I mean, in light of all the other connections and all."

"Now, do you really think I would have my men try to kill you over this?"

"The world of espionage is a dangerous game. Sometimes people are in the game and they don't even know that they're playing. And they don't know the rulebook."

"But you do."

"That's right, I do. And I also know when I'm not getting the whole truth."

"You know as well as I do that I can't reveal sensitive information."

"I'm not asking you to. I'm just asking that I be let in on what's going on. Because if I start digging deeper into this, and I find out that I'm being lied to, or I start being followed, or I start being led in a different direction, I'm gonna be very unhappy. And I don't want any bad blood to come out of this."

"Or spilled blood."

"That too," Bridge said.

"Luke, Gary Abbott did not work for us. We did not kill him. I do not know who did. And we did not shoot at you last night. All of that is the truth."

"The whole truth or just a version of it?"

"The version that I can reveal." Pinnacle One then stood up and put his sunglasses on. "It's been good talking to you, Luke. If you find anything else of interest on this case, I'd appreciate you filling me in on it."

"You can count on it."

Bridge sat there as he watched his former boss walk away. As the man did so, his other men fell in behind him as they walked back to their car. Once they were completely out of sight, Nicole came over to the fountain and sat down next to her boyfriend.

"Hear all that?" Bridge asked.

"Sure did."

"What'd you think?"

"I think he's lying."

"About which part?"

"Most of it. Maybe he's telling the truth about Abbott not being an agent. I'm not sure about that. But I think he knows a lot more than he's saying."

"Question is how long it takes us to prove it."

"I can prove some of it right now."

"How?"

"Well, I can't say for sure whether he's the one behind us being shot at last night. And I can't say whether he had Abbott killed. And I can't say for sure whether he's behind the disappearance of that PI."

"Then what can you say?"

"I can definitely say he knows about Bevell."

"How?"

"You remember that guy we fought with the blond hair? The one who put you through the table?"

Just hearing it brought back bad memories for Bridge. He put his hand on his back as if he were still feeling the pain. "I'm not likely to forget it anytime soon."

"That guy's one of Pinnacle One's guards."

Bridge was astonished. "What?"

"Yeah. He was standing up there on the terrace. I didn't notice him at first when I was there. But when I walked around and stood by the trees on the side there after they showed up, I noticed him."

"You sure it was him? The same guy?"

"Positive. I'd recognize him anywhere. So unless he's acting on his own, I'd say there's one guy who sent him to Bevell's house."

"Pinnacle One."

"Which means that he knows him. And he knows more of what's going on."

Bridge sighed. "I'm pretty sure I hate this case."

"Not too late to back away from it."

"Yes, it is. We're already into it."

"But not so far where we can't go back. I mean, it's not like we've got some pivotal information that we're not acting on. We still don't know much."

"But we know enough," Bridge said. "We know things don't add up. And we know there's a brother out there who wants answers. And he's not gonna give up until he gets them. And if he keeps on, without our help, he has no idea what he's dealing with. You know as well as I do what's likely to happen to him and whoever else he brings in if it's not us."

"There's gonna be more dead bodies."

Bridge nodded.

"If we keep going... I just hope we're not joining them."

Bridge took a deep breath, then flipped his lips together and blew air through his mouth. "Yeah."

"Where do we go from here?"

Bridge took a few seconds to think about it. "We need to dig deep. Deep into Gary Abbott's background. If he really wasn't an agent and they were just using him to facilitate information quietly, there should be some trails we can follow. He wouldn't be good enough to cover everything up."

"Unless they wiped everything away."

"Let's get Eric in on this. Maybe he can tell us something."

"What about Chris?" Nicole asked. "Should we tell him his brother was involved with the CIA or wait?"

"I think the sooner we tell him what's going on the better it'll be. For him."

Nicole agreed. "Yeah. If he knows what he's up against, maybe he'll be a little more cautious about what he does. Like breaking into houses."

"That's the hope. If not... if not, he'll end up where his brother is."

6

With Bridge and Nicole back at the hotel, he immediately called Chris Abbott to let him know his brother was into some other things, things he couldn't explain, and things Abbott wouldn't understand. While Bridge was on the phone with him, Nicole called their trusty FBI friend Eric Happ, putting him on the video line.

"Oh no, it's been a few weeks," Happ said. "What do you want?"

"Can't a girl just call to say hi to her friend?"

"I think you used that line on me for the model kidnapping case."

"I did?"

"Pretty sure."

"Oh. I'm gonna have to start working on new material."

Happ laughed. "Probably would be a good idea.

'Cause every time you come at me with the same line, I automatically know what you want."

"I'll work on it."

"At least keep me guessing for a few minutes."

"Noted."

"So what do you want? Luke making you do his dirty work? Figured I'd have a harder time saying no to you?"

Nicole looked toward the hallway, but Bridge was in the bedroom and out of sight. "Uh, no, he's just... busy with someone else."

"Oh, you have competition now?"

"Don't be ridiculous. He knows I would kill anyone else who even looked at him."

Happ laughed again. "So what's up?"

"We caught... something. It's a big one."

"Uh oh."

"Yeah. I think we might be dealing with some... agencies on this one."

"As in ours?"

"Or those similar to yours."

"You talking about your former friends and colleagues?"

Nicole nodded. "Yeah."

"So what are you coming to me for? You guys are still tight with them, aren't you?"

"Well, I wouldn't say tight. It's not adversarial. Even so, what can I do?"

"We would like to know if you have anything on a guy named Gary Abbott," Nicole said.

"Agent?"

"Well, he's dead now. Been that way for a year."

"I don't understand."

Nicole then went over the entire case with him to catch him up. After getting the full rundown, Happ sighed and shook his head.

"I don't know if I wanna be messing around with this thing."

"C'mon, Eric, he's not an agent. At least as far as we know. He's a dead U.S. citizen who has a brother that wants answers. I mean, he's been gone for a year and the police have nothing."

"You think they got pressured not to look into it?"

Nicole shrugged. "I don't know. Maybe they really had no leads and had nowhere to go. But if that's the case, that points to people even higher up who know how to avoid these kinds of things."

"Nic, I know you and Luke mean well with these things, and I'm usually always right there to support you..."

"But?"

"But if this thing leads up to somewhere that it shouldn't... you could be walking into you don't even know what."

"I know."

"If, just for the sake of argument, this guy really

was killed by the CIA, in this country, you know what kind of shit-storm you're going to create?"

Nicole sighed. "I know. But if he wasn't, then we'll have let a killer go scot-free."

"You guys are just compelled to look into this, aren't you?"

Nicole nodded. "We are."

"I hope you know what you're doing."

"Me too."

"And I hope you're prepared for whatever happens as a result of it."

"We are."

"All right. Well, I guess give me some time to look into it, and I'll get back to you."

"Thanks, Eric. You're the best."

"I know. It's nice hearing you say it though."

After getting off the line with Happ, Nicole went back to work on the computer, trying to dig up as much information as she could on Abbott. Then, whenever Happ got back to her, she could compare what he had against what she had and see if there were any discrepancies or something new that she either overlooked or didn't have access to, which was always possible when looking into someone who had done business with the government. About twenty minutes later, she looked over and saw Bridge coming out of the bedroom. He had his hands on his head, puffing air through his lips, and he looked stressed..

"Didn't go so well?" Nicole asked.

Bridge came into the living room, plopped down in a chair, and rubbed the top of his head. "Uh, well, I guess it went OK."

"Doesn't look it."

"Well, explaining that your brother was secretly doing business with the CIA has a tendency to... uh, well... it tends to be hard to understand and accept."

"I can understand that."

"And when everything you say tends to create even more questions with no answers, it can be overwhelming."

"For him or for you?"

"Both."

Nicole went back to working on the computer, but after a couple of minutes, stopped typing and turned back to her boyfriend. "What's your gut say on this?"

Bridge thought for a few seconds, taking a few deep breaths before answering. "Honestly, my gut says that I don't think the agency is involved in his killing. I just... if he's a natural salesman who goes overseas a lot, if the agency wanted to do him in, they probably could have done it a lot easier, without so many questions, and without anyone really looking into it in a foreign country. It would have been easier to explain. You know, he got mugged, went to a wrong part of town, car accident, whatever. And nobody probably would've thought twice about it. But if you kill him here, people like PIs, or us, start looking into things, and you've got a mess on your hands."

Nicole agreed. "It would be easier to kill him over there."

"Yeah, so, it doesn't make sense to do it here if that's what their intentions were."

"Maybe they were caught off guard by his murder as much as everyone else was, and whatever they were working on, they had to distance themselves from it for whatever reason."

"That would make sense. At least as much as anything else at this point."

"And that's not even taking Bevell into account yet," Nicole said. "Where's he?"

"I can tell you where he probably is, but you wouldn't like it."

"At the bottom of a hole?"

"Question is, whose hole? The agency's or whoever killed Abbott?"

"Assuming it's not one and the same."

"Yeah." Bridge let out a few more sighs, hating the case with each second that passed. Even still, he was involved now. He wasn't giving up on it.

"I guess it could be worse."

"No, it couldn't."

"Could be in Mexico."

"To be honest, and I know this is gonna shock you, but I think I'd rather be there right now."

Nicole pulled her head back like she was shocked. "No, you didn't."

"Oh, I did."

"No, you didn't."

"I did."

"You know, I'm gonna remind you of that the next time we have to go back there."

"Hopefully there won't be a next time."

"There's always a next time."

"No, there's not."

"Always is a next time. For everything."

"I disagree."

"Name something," Nicole said.

"If you're already dead, there's no next time. Unless, of course, they dig up your body and start shooting you again. Though I guess technically you're still dead from the first time, so you still can't be killed again. Right?"

"Funny."

"Well, I was just saying."

"How 'bout if you say something intelligent about this case?"

"Eh, can't help you with that one. You talk to Eric?"

"Yeah, he's gonna look into it and get back to us. What do you wanna do next?"

"Well, we already know that Abbott was working with the agency, right? So I don't think it'd do much good to retrace his steps from the first time that happened up to now, would it?" Bridge said.

"I dunno. Maybe."

"It'd probably be better to work backwards, wouldn't it? Figure out what he'd been doing recently and go from there. Because whatever happened to him, I think it's safe to say it's because of whatever he was doing recently and not something he was working on three years ago. If that was the case, he would have been killed then."

"Makes sense. Should we try to simultaneously work on finding the PI too?"

Bridge got up and went over to the table, picking up Bevell's planner. There were a few leads in there he wanted to check out. There were a couple of names, dates, and times in the couple of days leading up to his disappearance that Bridge wanted to look into.

"I'll look into this stuff," Bridge said, holding up the planner. "You keep on Abbott."

"You gonna check that stuff out alone?"

Bridge shrugged. "What could possibly happen?"

"You really need an answer to that?"

"Uh, no."

They spent two more hours working, with Nicole trying to piece together every little detail of Abbott's life in the months leading up to his death. Bridge tried to figure out who the names were in Bevell's planner. There were two names on it, but he didn't think they went together. They could have been first or last names, though one sounded more like a nickname. One was Kenny. The other was Stash. Bridge's concentration was broken when his phone started ringing again. He wasn't sure if he should have been happy or not to see Happ's name on his screen.

"Hey, Happy, what's up?"

"Nicole told me about the case you guys are on."

"Yeah?"

"She mentioned something about a PI that went missing."

"Yeah?"

"A guy named Bevell? Is that right?"

"Right so far."

"Darren Bevell?"

"That's him."

"Well, he's not missing anymore."

"Oh. He turned up?"

"Um, well, sort of. He's dead."

"What are the details?"

"Uh, really aren't any that I can tell so far. Just got word that he was found by the police roughly an hour or two ago."

"Can't say that I'm surprised," Bridge said. "I was figuring this call would come sooner or later."

"Nicole gave me the details on everything earlier and uh... it's a little strange."

"In what way?"

"The police believe that Bevell's body was moved from wherever he was originally killed to the place where he was dumped."

"They pretty sure of that?"

"Seem to be," Happ replied. "There was no blood at the scene. And there's something else."

"What's that?"

"His body was discovered in the same alley that Gary Abbott's was."

"Seriously?"

"How's that for coincidences?"

"Heavy."

"There's one more thing," Happ said.

"What?"

"I don't know if it's just a coincidence or not, but..."

"When someone starts a sentence with those words, it's usually not."

"Yeah, well, he was killed with two bullets to the chest."

"And?"

"So was Gary Abbott."

Bridge let out a loud sigh. "OK."

"I can already hear the frustration mounting, Luke."

"Not because of what it is. More like because of what it might be."

"It's got agency ties written all over it."

"Yeah."

"You think they know what's going on?" Happ asked.

"That's my hunch. I'm not sure they're behind it, but I think they know. Or at least have an idea. Maybe they know who's behind it and are looking for them too. I don't know. But I know there's something going on here. There's something rotten in the state of Denmark."

"I hear you."

"Where does that saying come from anyway?" Bridge asked. "Do you know? Is Denmark a smelly place or something?"

"Uh, no. As far as I know, Denmark's a beautiful place."

"Where's that line come from then?"

"I believe it was a line in a Shakespeare play. *Hamlet*, I think."

"Oh. I guess you can tell I'm not a Shakespeare guy then, huh?"

"Yeah, it kind of shows."

"Hmm. Interesting."

"Not as interesting as what you got going on right now."

"Yeah, tell me about it."

"You got any other leads?" Happ asked.

"Looking into someone named Kenny and someone named Stash. They were in Bevell's planner the day before he went missing. I don't know if they have anything to do with this or not. But I guess it needs checking."

"Kenny and Stash?"

"Yeah, you know them?"

"Not offhand, but I can do some checking on my end too."

"Thanks, I appreciate that."

"No problem. Luke?"

"Yeah?"

"I told Nic earlier, so I guess I'll tell you now."

"What's that?"

"You need to be careful on this."

"I know."

"Even if it's not the agency behind this, then it's a sure thing they know who is. And if whoever it is is taking people out for whatever reason, it's also probably a sure thing that you're now on their radar. And if you're not yet, the more you dig into it, you will be soon."

"I know."

"You be careful."

Bridge tried to sound more upbeat. "You know me, I'm the agent of caution."

Happ faked a cough. "Uh, yeah, right. More like the agent of incaution."

"Is that even a word?"

"Of course it is. You think I'd use a word if it wasn't one?"

"I dunno. Maybe."

"It's a word."

"I'll take your word for it."

"Can we just stop with the merry-go-round?"

Bridge tried to make light of it, but he appreciated his friend's words of advice. "I'll be careful."

"Good. 'Cause I'd hate to see your name cross my desk in an unflattering way."

"You mean there's been a flattering way?"

"All right, all right, I'm done. Talk to you later."

The smile from Bridge's face after teasing his friend was quickly wiped away after he put his phone away and thought of everything that he was just told. Nicole was kind of listening in, though she couldn't decipher everything that had gone on. Judging by the look on Bridge's face, it wasn't good.

"What's happened?"

"They found Bevell's body," Bridge answered. "Same spot as Abbott's."

"Same exact spot?"

"Same spot."

"Wow. That's not a coincidence."

"No, it's not."

"Guess we don't need to bother looking for him anymore."

"No." Bridge then looked at the planner again. "But we can find out if these names mean anything."

"And if they do?"

Bridge looked at the planner again, then his eyes went over to the locked cabinet that he kept his gun in. "Then I'd say business is about to pick up."

7

Bridge felt his body shake. His eyes flickered, and he saw flashes of light slip through the cracks of the curtains. He turned over on his side, away from the outline of his girlfriend, who was standing next to the bed.

"C'mon, Luke, wake up."

"Awe, not now, Nic, please. I'm tired."

"I want you for something."

"Please, not now. I promise I'll give it to you later."

"No, not that. Well, wait, promise?"

"I promise." Bridge started drifting off to sleep again.

Nicole furiously shook his body to wake him again. "It's important, Luke."

"Nic, please. I promise I'll give it to you later. Twice, if you want."

"Oooh. That's nice. Can we do one in the shower?"

"Sure." Bridge's voice was groggy. In order to go back to sleep, he would have given in to just about anything at that moment. "Whatever you want."

"I love it when you're like this." Bridge's eyes closed again, waking up a few seconds later upon feeling his girlfriend's hands on his shoulder. "Can we get kinky with the second one?"

"Fine. Whatever you want. Just let me go back to sleep."

"What about on the kitchen counter or something?"

"Uh... whatever. Just let me sleep."

Nicole was happy with the bargaining session, though it really wasn't what she came in there for. But it was a win all the same. She thought about continuing to try to get Bridge up, but she didn't want to seem like she had tricked him into giving her their later love-making sessions. So she left the room for five minutes. It was just long enough for him to feel like he went back to sleep for a while. She came back in and lightly shook her boyfriend's body. Bridge started to stir again.

"Awe, c'mon, Nic, I gave you everything you wanted already."

"Come on, Luke, I let you sleep for an extra hour."

Bridge's eyes suddenly flashed wide open. "You did?"

"Yes. I was last in here an hour ago."

"Wow, it feels like it was only five minutes."

"Well, it wasn't. It's now eight fifteen. Time to get up."

Bridge sat up and stretched his arms out. He yawned, then leaned over to give his lovely girlfriend a kiss. "Thanks for letting me sleep that extra hour."

Nicole faked a cough. "Oh, yeah, no problem. Feel better?"

"Yeah, I think I really needed that extra time."

"Well, you deserved it."

"Thank you."

"Don't forget what you agreed to later."

"Wait. What?"

"For letting you sleep extra, you agreed to a few of my suggestions."

Bridge batted his eyes. He kind of sort of remembered something, though he was fuzzy on the details. "What did I agree to?"

"Two little sessions later on tonight."

"Little sessions?"

Nicole grinned at him seductively. "Well, we'll see how little it is."

Bridge closed his eyes and slumped his head, wondering what he had agreed to. "Oh, boy."

"It'll be great. One will be in the shower. Nothing unusual." Bridge made a face, suggesting it wasn't so bad. "The other will be on the kitchen counter."

"Wait, the kitchen counter?"

"If you want to keep things fresh and alive, Luke,

you have to be willing to experiment with different things."

"Are you sure I agreed to this?"

"Yep."

Bridge put his hand on the side of his head like he had a headache coming on. "I think I need some aspirin."

"It'll be fine. You'll love it."

"We'll see."

"Anyway, none of that is why I came in here."

"It's not?"

"No. We've got news."

"You got a new sex toy in the mail?"

"Don't be funny." Nicole's concentration then slipped, thinking of a few other possibilities with her boyfriend. "Though that does give me a few ideas about—"

"Never mind." Bridge snapped his fingers. "Focus. What news?"

"Oh. That. Yeah, well, I figured out who those two names are."

"What names?"

Nicole looked up at the ceiling and rolled her eyes. "Are you still sleeping?"

"I honestly wish I was after this conversation."

"Kenny and Stash."

"Did Stash replace Cartman or Stan?"

"Don't be ridiculous. Will you stop fooling around so we can get down to business?"

"You talk about sex toys and different positions, and I'm the one fooling around?"

"You brought up the sex toy."

"I did?"

"Yes."

"Oh. See what you do to me."

Nicole couldn't resist the opportunity since she was wearing his shirt buttoned only at the bottom. She leaned forward and put her ample breasts into her boyfriend's face. Bridge, like always, couldn't resist her charm. After enjoying her body for a couple of minutes, he was finally able to pull away, thinking about what he assumed she came in there for.

"Wait, what about them?"

"Who?" Nicole asked.

"Business first."

"You promised."

"I didn't promise you anything in bed."

Nicole sighed as she pulled away. "You're such a buzzkill."

"You love me anyway."

"I do. But why can't you just enjoy the moment."

"Because you were going to tell me something."

"I was?"

Bridge snapped his fingers again. "Focus, Nicole, focus."

She put her hands on his crotch. "I am focusing."

"On business."

"This is business for me."

"Oh my god, you're impossible."

"But you love me, anyway."

Bridge smiled. "I do." He gave her another long and passionate kiss that he hoped would satisfy her long enough that they could finally get back to their original business. "Our business-business first. Then our personal business later."

Nicole sighed again. "Fine." She pulled the covers off of his naked body and admired his form. "I love it when you sleep like that."

"Well, I don't have much of a choice when you wake me up for some extra activity in the middle of the night."

Nicole smiled. "That was fun, though, wasn't it?"

"It was."

"You should sleep like this more often. Even if we aren't doing anything."

"If you finally tell me about Kenny and Stash, I'll think about it."

"Will you do it tonight?"

"Am I not on the hook for enough things later?"

Nicole shrugged. "Don't you like to make me happy?"

"I do."

"Well then?"

"Why is everything like a bargaining session for sex with you?"

"Because I love sex. I love you. And I love putting

the two together. Would you prefer if I took my needs elsewhere?"

"Of course not. Wait, would you?"

"Don't be stupid." Nicole leaned forward and started kissing him again. "You know you'll be the only man who's ever good enough for me."

They kept kissing before Bridge was finally able to remove his lips from hers. "Wait, wait, wait. See, you're doing it again."

"What?"

"Everything just always turns into... you know."

"Why do you say it like it's a bad thing?"

Bridge put his hand on his head again. His headache was now fully formed. "Now my head really does hurt."

"You want some aspirin?"

Bridge nodded. "Yes."

Nicole went into the bathroom to get the aspirin bottle. Bridge admired her tanned legs, which were totally visible since she was only wearing one of his dress shirts. Though he often sounded like he was complaining about her sex-crazed ways, he usually didn't mind. He actually liked that she was like that. He just had to sometimes rein her in and keep her focused.

She walked back in a minute later with some aspirin and a glass of water.

"When'd you get that dress?"

Nicole laughed. "Like it?"

"I do. Looks better on you than me."

"Doesn't everything?"

"True." After Bridge downed the aspirin and water, he desperately tried to get the conversation back on track. "Now, can we talk about Kenny and Stash?"

"Oh. Yeah, I guess so. If that's more interesting than me."

"It's not. But we really need to figure out what's going on here. Besides, you are booked for two sessions later."

"I guess so."

"What'd you find out?"

"Kenny's full name is Gregory Kenny."

Bridge looked away for a second, tilting his head as he let the name go through his memory bank. "Gregory Kenny. Why does that name sound familiar?"

"Usually goes by the name Greg Kenny."

Bridge whispered it again. "Greg Kenny. It feels like I know the name, but I can't place it."

"Maybe you know it because he's an ex-CIA agent."

"He was an agent?"

"Yep."

Bridge kept thinking about the name, then suddenly snapped his fingers. "Greg Kenny. Now I remember him."

"You do?"

"He worked out of a few European stations. I crossed paths with him in Russia and in Ukraine. I didn't realize he was out of the game."

"Well, out of that game maybe. Seems like he might be in this one."

"How so?"

"According to all the records I was able to get my hands on, Kenny left the agency about a year ago."

"On good terms?"

"Eh, doesn't look like it."

"What happened?"

"That I can't say for sure. There's a ton of information about him that's been redacted and is still listed as classified. I don't have the clearance to get into it, and it's too encrypted for me to hack into it."

Bridge was silent for a few moments as he thought about things. "Wait, he left a year ago?"

"Yep."

"Same time as when Abbott was found dead."

"Kenny left the agency exactly two weeks before that."

"Huh. That can't be a coincidence."

"Probably not."

"Where's he at now?"

Nicole shrugged. "Don't know. Agency doesn't know either, apparently. They've got an alert out on him that if anyone runs into him or finds him, they're to call it in immediately."

"He's definitely not on good terms then. They only do that for people they want off the street."

"How's he figure into all this?"

"Well, I'm kind of assuming it involves Stash."

"Who's he?"

"He's on the agency's hit list."

"Why?"

"Associating with known terrorists, illegal arms dealing, trafficking, I guess you can take your pick of which."

"An all-around bad guy."

"Seems like."

"What have we gotten ourselves into here?"

"I'm just guessing," Nicole said, "but maybe we've fallen into a case of a rogue CIA agent who's in bed with a criminal who's selling illegal arms to people who are even worse than he is."

Bridge nodded. It sounded as good as any other theory they'd come up with since they'd started this case. "Should I also assume that Stash isn't his real name?"

"You shouldn't. I can't find out what his real name is. He's apparently just known as Stash. First name, last name, nickname, I don't know."

"Is he American, European, what?"

"Sure."

"Nobody knows?"

"That's apparently the gist of it. They know the name. Don't know the face."

"So I take it nobody knows whether he's here or abroad."

Nicole pointed at him. "You're correct."

"And Kenny? Is he here?"

"They believe he's in America, probably on the East Coast, though they can't exactly pin it down at the moment."

"He's probably got so many fake passports and aliases it'll make your head spin."

"Don't you?"

"Well... that's different."

"You use your powers for goodness instead of evil?"

"That's right."

They sat there together thinking for the next several minutes, though only one of them was thinking about the situation with Abbott. With the sheets only halfway up Bridge's thigh, Nicole was doing some thinking—and admiring—about some other things. Bridge finally threw the sheets off entirely and stood up, Nicole putting her hands on both sides of his lower half. Bridge stood there, enjoying what she was doing, though he closed his eyes and sighed, knowing he had to proceed. He put his hand on hers and somehow was able to find the strength to take it off of him.

"Business first."

Nicole sighed, and her shoulders slumped. She shook her head. "The only man in America who would do this. Everybody else would happily let whatever happens happen. But not you. Oh no. You have to be professional all the time."

Bridge smiled, grabbing his phone off the nightstand. "If it makes you happy, I'll stand here naked while I make my call."

Nicole grinned. "Oh, that'll make me happy." She began fondling him again as he dialed the number.

Bridge tried to block out what he was feeling as he began talking. "This is Alpha One-Two-Seven-Six-Five."

"What is your business?"

"I need to speak to Pinnacle One. Tell him it's important."

"Hold on."

Nicole pulled him down onto the bed and began working him over as Bridge kept the phone pressed to his ear. He hoped he wasn't going to be put on hold long, as he couldn't be sure how long he could hold out from the pleasant feelings that were happening to him. Luckily, it was less than a minute.

"Pinnacle One will see you in one hour at the location of your previous meeting."

Bridge cleared his throat as he took a deep breath. "Uh... better make that two hours."

"Very well. I will let Pinnacle One know two hours."

As soon as the line went dead, Bridge dropped the phone from his hand, letting it fall onto the floor.

"What happened to later?" Bridge asked.

"I'm calling one of them in now. What are you meeting with them about again?"

Bridge tried to keep his thoughts clear, though it was tough to do so. "Uh... what?"

"You're meeting with P-One again?"

"Oh. I have more information to present this time. If he thinks I know more, and we're working on the same side, and I can help him, maybe he'll be more forthcoming this time."

"Someone else is going to be more forthcoming. Right now."

"Oh, boy."

8

Just as he did the last time he met Pinnacle One, Bridge was sitting on the ledge in front of the Bethesda Fountain. It was a little busier than the last time they were there. A few more kids, a few more parents with their strollers, a few more eyeballs. Right after Bridge looked at his watch, he saw his guests arrive. They came down the same steps as the last time; the guards moving over to the side, while some watched from the patio area. There was no need for small talk this time. Pinnacle One immediately took a seat next to Bridge, looking at his surroundings as he always did to make sure there were no uninvited guests.

"I must say, I was surprised to hear from you again so soon. It's been what, two days?"

"I like to work fast," Bridge replied.

"Yes, that's always been your reputation. So what

are we doing here again? You have something else for me?"

"You might say that. Or you might be able to give me something."

"Like what?"

"Like the truth about what's going on here."

"Luke, we've already had that conversation."

"No, you had it. Now you're gonna listen to what I have to say."

"I don't have to."

"But you will," Bridge said.

"What makes you think so?"

"Because you don't want to be burned, do you?"

"In what way?"

"You told me you didn't know the PI I was talking about, Darren Bevell."

"That's right, I don't."

"You're lying. You know him and I can prove it."

Pinnacle One shrugged. "And where's this going?"

Bridge tapped on his earpiece. "Go ahead and send it."

His former boss became slightly alarmed at knowing there was someone else out there that was unaccounted for. He started to squirm and thought about going back to his guards.

Bridge could see that he was getting antsy. "Just relax. There's nobody out there other than my associate."

"That doesn't exactly make me feel better, knowing

who your associate is. I hear you and Nicole have become more than just business associates."

"How'd you find that out?"

"Do you really have to ask? Knowing her proficiency and love for guns, not seeing her makes me a little nervous."

"Just relax. She's just sending me a picture."

Bridge then looked at his phone and saw the message from Nicole coming through. There he was. Nicole had taken a picture of the blond-haired man from their encounter at Bevell's house. He was still standing guard by the patio on this encounter too. Pinnacle One continued to look around, trying to locate Bridge's girlfriend, though her disguise seemed to one-up him. Bridge immediately held the phone up to show Pinnacle One the picture of his employee.

"Know him?"

Pinnacle One's gaze rose above the phone to where the man was standing. It wasn't hard to see, due to the background, that the photo had been taken in the last few minutes.

"I guess denying it at this point would do no good."

"Well, you could," Bridge said. "Be pretty foolish, though."

"So? He's one of my guards."

"He also happens to be the man we ran into at Bevell's house the other day. Dressed in black, mask, also a pretty good fighter. I got first-hand experience with that. And a few bruises to go along with it."

"Was he at Bevell's? I'll have to speak with him about that."

Bridge laughed. "Don't go there."

"Where?"

"Don't insult my intelligence by pretending he was somewhere without your knowledge and approval. Everything he does, from his morning trip to the bathroom to his lunch eating a Happy Meal, to his nine o'clock bedtime holding his teddy bear... it's all approved by you. Every second of his day has to be accounted for. Don't forget who you're talking to. I know it all. I know what it means."

Pinnacle One rubbed his cheek and his chin as he deliberated on whether he should reveal anything.

Bridge was getting a little frustrated with the runaround. "Dammit, Joe, I'm trying to help you. Stop giving me the brush-off and tell me what's going on here. I can help you if you let me, but if I'm left to freelance on this, then we both know I'm gonna step on some toes eventually, whether unintentionally or not. Help me sidestep that. I'm not some run-of-the-mill schmuck goofing off here. You know me. You know what I can do. I've never betrayed this agency and I still won't. But if you shut me out, my options will be limited."

Pinnacle One sighed. As much as he was trying to keep everything in-house, he knew Bridge could be trusted. Bridge had worked for him for a few years before he got assigned elsewhere.

"Yes. We were aware of Bevell's possible involvement in all of this."

"How was he involved?" Bridge asked.

Pinnacle One waived his hand in the air. "We don't know. As far as we could tell, he was just brought on a week or two ago. We were observing from a distance."

Bridge shook his phone slightly to bring attention back to the picture. "And this guy?"

"When I was told that Bevell had gone missing for a couple of days, I sent one of my men over to his house to see what he could find. I wanted to know if he had uncovered anything that would lead back to us."

"And that included killing us?"

"No." Pinnacle One put his finger in the air. "No. That was not him. After his encounter with you and Nicole, he fled the house and left the scene. Whoever shot at you afterwards was not him. It was not us. I would not have sanctioned that. Not yet, at least."

"Who was it then?"

"That I don't know. We've done some checking, but we've yet to come up with anything concrete."

"What's going on here?" Bridge asked.

Pinnacle One looked around again, making sure nobody was close enough to listen in. He took a couple of breaths before answering. "Gary Abbott was one of our assets. Due to his occupation of a traveling salesman, he was able to penetrate places that would have been tough for one of our known agents."

"I figured as much."

"We've used him often over the past few years. He was good. He provided us with a lot of information that we would not have known otherwise."

"And his death?"

"Shocking. We were as surprised as anybody. And it happening here was... unfathomable."

"His death or that it happened here?"

"Both."

"What was he working on?"

Pinnacle One sighed, not wanting to say. It was still top-secret information, and even though Bridge was friendly to the agency, and trustworthy, he was still now an outsider.

"Did it have anything to do with Greg Kenny or Stash?"

Pinnacle One snapped his head to the side and stared at Bridge.

"That look pretty much tells me that it does."

"Where have you heard those names?" Pinnacle One asked.

"I told you. I'm good at what I do."

"You've worked faster than even I had anticipated. I assumed that you would eventually come upon them, but I didn't think you would get those names for a few more weeks."

"Now, my intel says that Greg Kenny is a former CIA agent who left the agency two weeks before Abbott went missing. That's interesting in its own right, but the fact the agency now has an alert out on him, I don't think I'm too out of line thinking that the two are somehow connected."

Pinnacle One looked at him and sighed. "You sure you wouldn't like to come back to the agency and work for us?"

"I'm good where I'm at. I've also heard that Stash is a wanted fugitive with a sheet a mile long. How's it all tie together?"

"You've pretty much got it." Pinnacle One didn't see the use in trying to pretend or hide things anymore. Bridge probably had everything figured out now, anyway. "During the course of one of Abbott's trips overseas, he became privy to some information that suggested we had a mole on the inside."

"Kenny."

"Well, we didn't know who at the time. This was roughly two years ago. Stash has been on our radar for about three years now. We don't know much about him other than the name and what he does."

"Illegal arms?"

"Among other things. We suspect that he's got his hand in a variety of pots, including Iran, North Korea, Russia, pretty much everyone we've been at odds with."

"No real name?"

"No. We've used surveillance, informants, contacts, set up deals, everything you can think of; it's all been useless. He's evaded us at every turn."

"And Kenny? Where does he fit in?"

"We're not sure. We think he fits in on some level, though how much, we don't know."

"Why did he leave, and why is there an alert on him?"

"After Abbott discovered there may be a possible mole, we spent the next year trying to discover who that was. They hid themselves incredibly well. They left a few crumbs to follow, which we did, only to discover that they led nowhere."

"Maybe left false trails on purpose."

"Possibly. If he was aware we were on to him, he very well could have done it to throw us off the track and continue to disguise himself. Right up to his death, Abbott was on the road for about six months straight. He communicated to us that he needed a break. He wanted to come back home for at least a few weeks. We thought it was a good idea. Even though we were trying to find out who this traitor was, the man was not an agent, and we were afraid if he became tired, he may make some mistakes, slip up, and all our work would be thrown out the window."

"So he came home."

"He came home. One week after that he was found dead in an alley. And our best chance at finding that mole went out the window."

"So you never found out who it was?"

"No. Oh, we've had thousands of theories floating around. Some of them are possible, some of them are ridiculous and can be dismissed easily, and some of them are ridiculous, but they are still possible and cannot be ruled out."

"So where does Kenny come in?"

"Like you said, two weeks before Abbott came home, Kenny up and quit. He gave notice and said that he was cracking and couldn't handle it anymore."

"What were his assignments?"

"Critical. He was in deep. For the past few years he'd been working undercover, getting in deep with terrorist cells, criminal organizations, getting information on potential targets."

"So he was basically permanently in the field?"

"Yes. Everyone thought he was indispensable before he left. He was fluent in five languages, passable in five more, and was instrumental in several successes that we've had around the world."

"Is he the mole?" Bridge asked.

"At the time, we didn't think so. There was no chatter about him that we could uncover. We just assumed he was a man who finally cracked under the pressure of living a dangerous life. You know as well as I do that it happens sometimes."

"What about now?"

"Now we're not sure what to think. Right before Abbott came home, one of Kenny's aliases popped up on the radar here in New York. We looked for him, though we couldn't find him. A few days after Abbott was killed, Kenny's name popped up again, then he dropped off the map. So we know he was here at the same time as when Abbott was killed, we just don't know why."

"He's involved."

"Yes, well, that's one of the theories, and probably a good one, but we haven't been able to prove it yet. Or find out where the man is now. That's why there's an alert out on him. We want to question him to find out if he was the mole, if he was involved in Abbott's death, and what he's been doing for the past year."

"No idea if he's still here or not?"

"None. The fact is that men like him are even more dangerous than others. Because he lived a double life for so long, he's accustomed to living a lie, blending in, creating false identities, and he's had a long time to perfect that craft."

"Is he involved with Stash?"

"Not that we can determine. In all the information we've ever received on Stash, Kenny's name has never popped up. Though I guess it still is possible they may have interacted under different names, especially if Kenny thought he was being watched, but we haven't gotten any information that indicates that that is the case. But as always, it's possible until it's proven otherwise."

"If Kenny was the mole, and he killed Abbott because he thought he might be getting too close, then it's likely he also killed Bevell for looking into it."

"There's nothing to suggest the PI knew anything either."

"He didn't have to," Bridge said. "If Kenny got wind of him looking into things, whether he was close or not, he might have just killed him so he didn't have to worry about it."

"What difference would it make now? If Kenny was the mole, he's gone now, why would he care what the PI found out?"

"I suspect that Bevell found something. What it was, I'm not sure. Probably stumbled into it without knowing what it was is more likely, but I found both Kenny and Stash's name in Bevell's planner. He didn't just come up with those names out of a hat. He found them somewhere."

"You found their names in his planner?"

"I did. Now, that means they're linked together somehow. I'm not sure how or why, but they're involved."

"That certainly puts a spin on things."

"It does."

"I know you're going to keep working on this, Luke, and I'm good with that. I'm actually kind of glad that you are. But I would appreciate a heads-up if you find anything out."

"Well, I guess that would depend."

"On?"

"On whether it's a two-way street. I don't mind getting involved. But I like to know I'm not getting played for a sucker."

"I give you my word that if we find anything out on this, you'll know about it."

The two men shook hands.

"Good enough for me," Bridge said.

"Besides, since we don't operate domestically, we need someone on the ground here who can work on our behalf."

Bridge grinned. "Yeah. It would be helpful, though, if you could give me everything you have on Kenny, Abbott, and Stash. Tough to operate when you don't have all the facts."

Pinnacle One hesitated for a second, not sure about opening up their files, but he eventually relented. He knew to have a man like Bridge on the job, helping them, he needed all the information. "You'll get them. I'm not sure it'll do you any good, but you'll get them. We've been all over their files a few dozen times. It's never gotten us anywhere."

"Maybe you need a fresh pair of eyes."

"Maybe so. I will have their files sent over to you in the next few hours."

"I appreciate that."

Pinnacle One then stood up, Bridge doing the same. "We'll keep plugging away at it."

Bridge nodded. "I'll do the same."

"Oh, before I go, how 'bout an introduction to your better half? You met her after you left us, did you not?"

"I did."

Bridge thought about it for a second, wondering if

he actually wanted to have Nicole show herself physically. P-One already knew what Nicole looked like. He'd looked at the files, that was obvious through some of his comments. But looking through files was one thing. Seeing someone in person was another. Bridge finally decided to bring her in. In the end, he figured it really didn't matter much. It wasn't as if he was trying to keep her a secret. If that were the case, he would have kept it up. But Nicole was a known entity. There really wasn't much point in trying to hide her. Bridge looked to his right and waved for Nicole to come in. She was dressed in a similar fashion as the last time. Sneakers, shorts, tank top, a hat, and sunglasses. She cautiously approached the pair, taking her sunglasses off as she got near them. Bridge was about to introduce the two of them before Pinnacle One cut him short.

"I don't believe introductions are in order," Pinnacle One said. "So this is the woman who finally got you to settle down."

"That's her."

"Quite a feat, my dear."

"It has its challenges," Nicole said.

Pinnacle One smiled. "I'm sure it does. Judging by how you've eluded our eyes twice now, I can see how resourceful you are. Beauty and brains. A deadly combination."

"It is."

Pinnacle One smiled again as he looked over at

Bridge. He then leaned forward to whisper to Nicole. "You keep taking care of him. He'll need you."

Nicole returned the smile. "I know."

Pinnacle One nodded. "Next time don't be in the shadows." He then started walking away, putting his hand in the air, though he never turned around to look at them. "Until next time."

As they watched him and his men walk away, Nicole wondered where they would go from there. "What next?"

Bridge sighed. "I don't know. But we got our work cut out for us."

9

By the time Bridge and Nicole got back to their hotel room, Bridge had some new ideas. Nicole logged onto her computer and instantly found the files on Kenny, Stash, and Abbott had been emailed to them. While she started looking at them, Bridge called their FBI friend.

"What now?" Happ asked.

"New plan of attack."

"How's that?"

"Can you run camera footage from all locations near Bevell's house? If we can find the car that shot at us and run the plate, we can start unwinding this thing."

"Weren't you guys talking with your former friends about that?"

"We're in agreement that I'm going to help them."

"Really?"

"Well, they can't really operate here, right?"

Happ laughed. "Yeah."

"So they need someone who can."

"Which is you?"

"They trust me."

"And you trust them?"

"So far," Bridge replied. "We'll see how it goes, but right now, from everything I understand, they seem just as much in the dark about this as anybody. Seems to me they're looking for answers to questions they don't even have."

"Yeah. Oh, I checked out those names you gave me, Kenny and Stash? Nothing came up on our end for either of them."

"Yeah, I already got what I needed on them. Kenny is a former agent and Stash is on the agency's radar for arms trafficking, among other things."

"Wait, and you said you found their names in Bevell's planner?"

"Yep."

"How would he get that?"

"I don't know. But he must have run into someone who knew them. If you can find that car, that might help us get there."

"All right, give me the details."

Bridge then described the car as best he could remember along with the approximate time. It was a black four-door sedan. Looked new. Chrome wheels.

The back windows were tinted. He was pretty sure he'd know it if he saw it again.

"I'll start running it through and see if we get any hits," Happ said.

"Thanks. Let me know if you get anything."

"Will do."

Once Bridge was done, he went and joined his girlfriend in the living room and started examining the files of their subjects.

"Anything that jumps out at you so far?" Bridge asked.

"Not yet."

"I wouldn't bother going back too far. Whatever we're looking for should have happened in the last few years."

"You think we'll know it if we see it?"

"No."

"You said you knew Kenny?"

"Only briefly. We didn't go on any missions together or anything. We were in a couple of the same meeting rooms, bumped past each other, that sort of thing."

"Ever talk to him?"

"Just in passing. A few comments here or there. This mission sucks, that's not a good idea, that sort of thing. Never anything more than that. And it was maybe three times that I saw him. Wouldn't know anything more about him than what's in the files. I can't give any personal information as far as what makes him tick or things he likes to do if that's what you're wondering."

"Thought it was worth a shot."

They worked straight through for another hour, reading and analyzing every move that the men they were looking for had made in the past few years, at least as far as was documented. Their concentration was broken by the sound of Bridge's phone ringing. It was Happ.

Bridge looked at it. "It's Eric. Maybe he found something." He then put the phone to his ear. "Yo, Happster. What's up?"

"I hate those nicknames, you know."

"You love it. Gives you an identity."

"Really doesn't."

"I'll remember that."

"Will you?"

"No."

"I thought not."

"So what's up?"

"Check your email right now. I've sent you a few possibles for the car you're looking for. Let me know which one, if any, it is."

"All right, give me a second to get in there." Bridge went over to the table and went on his laptop.

"You know, it's harder to do these things over the phone and on a computer. Can't you just come in so I can show you all this in person?"

"Yeah, well, you know how I feel about that.

Nothing against you, you're fine, but you know I don't like going in that building."

"It's just an FBI building, Luke."

"Yeah, I know, maybe it's all the years I spent at the agency, but I just don't like going into government buildings anymore."

"It's not like anyone's waiting in the weeds to shoot you once you come in or anything."

"Yeah, well, you never know."

"You have a lot of hang-ups, you know that?"

"Maybe one or two."

"One or two? That's not what your girlfriend says," Happ said.

"What's she been telling you?"

"Not much. Just about Mexico, your problem with helicopters..."

"OK, that's enough."

"She also told me—"

Bridge got into his email just in time, since he didn't want to hear any more about his issues with anything. "OK, I'm in."

"OK. I sent you six different pictures. Let me know if your car is in there."

Bridge looked carefully at each picture. Two of the pictures he didn't need to look at very long as they weren't even close to the car he saw. They weren't as pitch-black as the color of the car. The other four were all close. But only two of them had the windows tinted, and only one of those had the chrome wheels that he remembered.

"It's number four."

"You sure?" Happ asked.

"Positive. That's it."

"OK. I thought so."

"Who's it belong to?"

"Well, we did get a plate number, and it comes back as belonging to a Marianne Werther."

"Who's that?"

"No criminal history. Records I have show that she's a freelance marketing consultant."

"Which means what exactly?"

"That she gives marketing advice, I guess?"

"Does that mean she travels around a lot?"

"Could be."

"Nothing nefarious showed up in your records?"

"Nothing at first glance. I didn't do a deep dive, though. There's nothing outstanding on her, she's not wanted, and she has no history. That doesn't mean nothing's there. Just means there's never been a reason for anyone to look yet."

"Well, there's a reason now," Bridge said. "Because if that's her car, then she's got some explaining to do as to why someone took shots at me. Can you send over what you got on her?"

"Yeah, give me a few minutes on that. You want me to go talk to her?"

"No, I'd rather do that myself."

"You might want some backup in case."

"I've got backup."

"I meant the federal kind."

"Maybe next time. Since she's a woman, it'd probably be a good idea to bring Nic along. She has a way of getting through to the opposite sex when I can't. If it's just two dudes there with her, and she's a smart enough criminal to never show up on anyone's radar, then she might not admit anything with us."

"You're taking a big leap there, aren't you? Just because it's her car doesn't mean she knows what's going on. Maybe she's out of the country. Maybe it was stolen. Maybe she lent it to her boyfriend for the night. Could be a lot of things."

"That's a lot of maybes there. But you forgot one."

"What's that?"

"Maybe she's involved."

"Yeah. Well, let me know if you need anything."

"Just the file."

"Sending it over."

Bridge hung up and sat there, waiting for the file on Werther to show up in his inbox.

"What about me?" Nicole asked.

"Huh?"

"I heard my name mentioned."

"Oh. Eric found the car that shot at us outside Bevell's place."

"And?"

"We're gonna go talk to the owner."

"We are?"

"Yep."

"Who is it?"

"Woman named Marianne Werther."

"She friend or foe?"

"Don't know. As of now, I'd say to be on your guard."

"Right. Foe."

"We'll see."

Bridge downloaded her file and looked at it. There were no obvious red flags. She used her passport a lot, traveling at least once or twice every month for the last few years. She'd been issued a few parking and speeding tickets, but none in the last five years. There was nothing in her package to suggest she was anything other than a regular person who may have gotten mixed up in something beyond her comprehension. They would find out soon enough.

Nicole got ready within a few minutes, and they left for Werther's place. She lived in a three-story end-unit condo in a nice neighborhood. As they pulled up in front of the house, their eyes were immediately drawn to a vehicle a couple of cars away.

"You see what I see?" Nicole asked.

"I see it."

"That's the car."

"It sure is."

"That means she's involved."

Bridge thought it was likely, but he wasn't ready to

say definitively yet. "Probably. Let's not jump to conclusions before talking to her."

"She's guilty."

"Now how do you know that?"

"Her car was used in a high-profile incident."

"Yeah? Could've been her boyfriend or something."

"If her boyfriend is out shooting people, I'm sure she's aware of what's going on."

"Not necessarily. History is littered with people who hid major secrets from their husbands, wives, girlfriends, whatever."

"Nobody lends their car out unless they know where a person's going."

"Well, maybe the guy lied to her and said he was going to the library or someplace else."

Nicole gave him a look and shook her head. "Trust me on this, Luke. She knows."

"How can you be so sure when you haven't even looked or talked to her yet?"

"Intuition."

"That's not a thing."

"It's a thing."

"It's not a thing."

"It's totally a thing."

"OK, whatever." Bridge got out of the car, mumbling to himself. "It's not a thing."

"I heard that. And it totally is."

Bridge put his fingers on the handle of his pistol, which was tucked into the back of his pants and covered by his shirt. As they walked toward the condo, he suddenly stopped.

"What?" Nicole asked.

"Are you packing?"

"Am I packing what?"

Bridge's eyes immediately went to her chest. "Well, uh, duh, the uh…" He then motioned to his side, trying to think of the word for a gun.

"I'm always packing."

"I can see that, I know. But, um…" Bridge motioned and pointed to her, then to him, then his side, then back to her. "I mean… um… the, uh… I meant…"

"You mean a gun?"

"Uh, yeah, that."

"It took you that long just to ask if I had a gun?"

"I got distracted."

"Obviously."

"Why do you look so beautiful all the time?"

Nicole smiled. "You're becoming a charmer."

Bridge smiled back. "I'm trying." They started walking again. "Seriously, though, are you packing?"

"What kind of question is that? Are you serious? I'm always packing. You know that."

"Good."

"Worried that I'm right, aren't you?"

"No," Bridge said.

"See, you got it in your mind that she's involved and maybe her boyfriend's up there with her and we're gonna get in a shootout, aren't ya?"

"No."

"Just admit it. You're following my intuition."

"No, I'm not. And it's still not a thing."

"It's still a thing and always will be. Just admit that I'm right."

"I'm not admitting anything yet," Bridge said. "I'm just making sure we have all our bases covered. If something happens up there, then I'll admit you're right."

"Promise?"

"We don't even know if she has a boyfriend."

"She does."

"How do you know?"

"The old intuition thing is kicking into high gear."

Bridge stopped and sighed as his girlfriend kept walking. "That's not a thing."

10

Nicole banged loudly on Werther's front door, drawing a look from her boyfriend.

"What?"

"You trying to wake up the neighborhood?" Bridge asked.

"It's the middle of the day. Everyone's awake."

"They certainly are now."

Nicole kept banging away. "Marianne Werther!"

"If you're trying to scare her away before she answers the door, you're really doing a good job of it."

"Her car's here. She's in there. I just want her to answer the door."

"Ever think that maybe she went for a walk? We do live in a city where that happens, you know."

"She's in there." Nicole banged away some more.

"Ever think that she is in there and maybe now

doesn't want to answer the door because she thinks there's a crazed lunatic banging on her door?"

Nicole slowly turned and looked at him. "Do you want to talk to her or not?"

"I do. Preferably without her already on edge and irritated with the people who almost knocked her door down."

"Well, then maybe she should answer it."

"Some people don't answer the door for strangers, you know."

Nicole was about to respond with another sarcastic comment, but they could hear someone moving around inside. Then they heard the door unlock. Then it opened. Standing there was Marianne Werther. She was fairly tall and thin, with long black hair. She appeared to be in her mid-thirties, though she had a youthful-looking face.

"Yes? Can I help you?"

"Ms. Werther?" Bridge asked.

"Yes. Who are you?"

"My name's Luke and this is my partner, Nicole."

"What do you want?"

"We'd like to talk to you about an incident that happened the other day."

"Are you the police?"

"No, we're sort of like, part of a joint task force with the FBI."

"Where are your credentials?"

"We're undercover. We don't have credentials."

Werther smiled. "Then I'm not talking to you."

She started closing the door, but was stopped when Bridge blocked it from shutting with his foot. "I can have my Special Agent Happ down here in five minutes, if that's what you prefer. Or you can just talk to us and we'll be out of here. If I call him, the process might be messier... and take a lot longer."

Werther sighed and opened the door wide again. "What is it that you want?"

"A couple of days ago your car was seen at the scene of a shooting."

"That's impossible."

"It is, huh?" Nicole said. "Well, it was. And we're the ones who saw it."

Werther didn't seem flustered at all. She gave a sort of shrug, seeming unconcerned. "You must've seen something else."

"Oh, it was your car all right," Bridge said.

"OK, well, if that's all..."

Bridge took a picture out of the folder he was carrying with him, showing her the car from the camera photo that Happ had sent him. "Looks a lot like yours, doesn't it?"

"There's a lot of cars that look like that. That's not proof."

Bridge reached into the folder and removed another picture. This one had a full picture of the license plate. He showed that one to Werther too. "How 'bout this one? That proof enough for you?"

Werther looked at the pictures and cleared her throat. She was trying to think of a good explanation.

"Mind if we come in and talk?" Nicole asked.

"No, no," Werther said, giving a nervous smile. "Sorry, the place is a mess, and I'm in the middle of cleaning it."

"About the car?" Bridge asked.

"I don't know anything about it."

"So that's the way you wanna play this thing? Ignorance?"

Nicole tapped her boyfriend on the arm. "She's not gonna tell us anything. Let's just sit on her and wait for the rest of the boys to get down here. We can get a warrant, search her place, then Happ can interrogate her downtown."

"Might be for the best."

"OK. Wait." Werther took a deep breath as she tried to think of a story. "OK. I don't know exactly what happened the other night. I wasn't driving the car."

"Who was?"

"My brother Mark."

"You loaned him the car?"

Werther closed her eyes and nodded. "Yes."

"Why?"

Werther shrugged. "I don't know. I've always had a soft spot for him. He's my younger brother, but he's constantly in trouble, always getting into something. He came to me the other night and asked if he could borrow my car for a few hours. I asked him what he needed it for, but he wouldn't tell me."

"So you gave it to him, anyway?" Nicole asked.

"Yes. Like I said, I have a hard time saying no to him."

"And he gave no indication what he needed it for?"

"No."

"How did he seem when he returned it?"

"I don't know. I didn't see him when he brought it back. I was already asleep. He put the keys through the mail slot on the door."

"Well, whoever was in this car shot at us, just outside the house of a private investigator named Darren Bevell," Bridge said. "That name ring any bells for you?"

Werther shook her head. "No."

"What would your brother be doing there?"

"I honestly don't know. He hangs around a lot of people who are bad for him. He just can't break away from them. I've tried to help him, but... it's just no use. He doesn't listen."

"Where would your brother be now?"

"I don't know. He moves around a lot."

"Well, where's he living?"

"Like I said, he moves around a lot. He goes from apartments to hotels to apartments to motels constantly. He's never in the same place for more than a week."

"So how do you talk?"

"Honestly, it's usually him calling me wanting a favor."

"What about the people he's mixed up with?" Nicole asked.

"I don't know their names."

Nicole asked her a few more questions, basically getting the same story from Werther. As they talked, Bridge carefully studied Werther's actions and mannerisms. She was good. Too good. She talked like someone who was trained in interrogation tactics. He knew that everything coming out of her mouth was a lie, but she said it so convincingly. A lesser trained person wouldn't have noticed or believed anything other than what she was saying. But Bridge knew. For one thing, according to her file, she had no brother. But she put on a good performance.

If they were going to get anything of value out of Werther, Bridge knew they were going to have to up the ante. They'd have to do what was usually frowned upon in their business. They would have to let people know they were coming.

"What about Greg Kenny?" Bridge blurted out.

"Who?"

"Greg Kenny. You know him?"

Werther grimaced and shook her head. "No. Sorry. Doesn't ring a bell."

"I got a picture of him too." Bridge held the picture for her. She took the picture and looked at it closely.

"No. Sorry. I've never seen him."

"Ever hear the name Stash before?"

"Stash?"

"Yeah."

"Is that like a nickname or something?"

Bridge shrugged. "Could be."

Werther shook her head again. "No. Never heard of him. You think they might be involved with my brother?"

Bridge took the photo back from her. "Possible."

"Well, if that'll be all?"

"I suppose for now."

A serious expression came over Werther's face. "I'm not going to wish you luck in finding my brother, but if he really was involved in shooting at you... I'm sorry. I'm glad you're not hurt."

"Thanks."

"I assume you're going to keep looking for him?"

"That's the plan."

"I know it's what you have to do and all, but if you could do me a favor, and try not to hurt him?"

"That'll be up to him," Nicole replied.

"I know. If you could just do what you can to help him... I'd appreciate it." It almost looked like Werther's eyes were beginning to tear up.

"Thanks for the help," Bridge said.

"Sure."

Bridge and Nicole turned around and walked down the steps. Once they reached the sidewalk, Bridge turned around to look at the door again. His eyes glanced at the windows, seeing a curtain move.

"I guess our next move is finding this brother," Nicole said.

"Nope."

"What do you mean, no?"

Bridge started walking back to the car. "She doesn't have a brother."

Nicole stood there, letting the words sink in. She then ran after him. "What do you mean she doesn't have a brother?"

"Eric sent me her file. She's an only child.."

"Then why did you let her ramble on like that and not call her out on it?"

"Strategy."

"You wanna let me in on it?"

They both got back into their car. "Pull out and then come back around the block."

"What for?"

"I want her to see that we're leaving."

"But we're not?"

"Nope."

"What are we doing?"

"We're gonna follow her."

"What makes you think she's going somewhere?"

Bridge looked at her and smiled. "Intuition."

"Oh, now who's the funny one?" Nicole started the car and pulled out into traffic, quickly driving down the road so she could double back. "You wanna tell me now what you're thinking?"

"If we called her out on not having a brother, she'd just clam up, right? I mean, she wasn't going to tell us anything."

"Yeah, but she'd know we were on to her."

"She knows that anyway. Did you see the performance she gave? She was very good. Like she'd been coached on how to do that."

"What are you saying?"

"That she's not what she appears to be. She's involved in something. Maybe she's an agent, maybe she's involved with Kenny and he taught her, I don't know. That story about her brother was just to throw us off the trail for a few hours."

"Giving her enough time to run."

Bridge nodded. "If I'm right, and she's deep into this, she knows her cover's blown. She can't stay there. She's gotta go to wherever her safe spot is."

"And we'll be there to follow."

"That's the plan."

"You know, sometimes you seem like you know what you're doing."

Bridge smiled. "Sometimes."

They came back around the block, parking a little way down the street, though they still had a view of Werther's condo. They only had to wait a few minutes. Just as Bridge had predicted, Werther jetted out of the home and ran to her car, quickly getting inside.

"Someone's got their hair on fire," Nicole said.

"We made her nervous. Now let's see who she goes to."

Werther peeled out of her parking spot, Bridge and Nicole following her, though they made sure to keep their distance. With Werther being as cool as she was under questioning, they didn't think it was a hard jump to believe that she knew when she was being followed if they weren't careful. Nicole made sure she was at least four cars behind as they drove. After driving for ten minutes, they still couldn't be sure where she was headed.

"Where do you think she's going?" Nicole asked.

"Anyone's guess at this point."

They continued driving for another forty-five minutes, though at this point, they thought they might have been spotted. They drove down several of the same streets multiple times.

"Think she spotted us?"

"Tough to say," Bridge said. "She's not acting like she's trying to lose us. She's probably being careful and following protocol. I'm sure she, and whoever else she's in with, has gone over this scenario before. All we can do is keep with her and see what happens."

And nothing did happen, at least for another twenty minutes. They were getting tired of all the driving, but eventually, they knew Werther would get to her destination.

"Hope this happens by sundown," Nicole said. "Or it's gonna cut into my sex time."

Bridge slowly turned his head. "Does your mind always go there?"

"Why do you ask like it's a bad thing?"

"I'm just asking."

"Well, I haven't had it in a while."

"You just had it this morning!"

"Well, for me that's a while." Bridge put his hand on his forehead and rubbed it. Nicole briefly looked at the back seat. "I guess in a pinch we could do it back there if we had to."

Bridge turned his attention back to the cars in front of them, wanting to get out of that conversation as quickly as possible. Finally, after another ten minutes of aimlessly driving around, it appeared that Werther had come to where she was headed. She pulled over in front of an expensive-looking house and parked her car. Nicole instantly pulled over as well, much further down and hopefully out of sight.

"So who do you think this is?" Nicole asked.

They watched Werther get out of her car and walk toward the house, where the front door opened, revealing a man standing there and waiting for her. Nicole reached for one of their folders.

"Is that Kenny?"

"That's not him," Bridge replied.

"Well, who is it?"

"I don't know."

"Maybe it's that Stash guy."

"Guess anything's possible."

"Maybe we should go in for a closer look," Nicole said.

"Let's just give it some time first. If they've initiated their run package, they might not be here for long."

Nicole looked at the time. "Twenty minutes."

"Thirty."

"Twenty."

"Thirty."

"Twenty-five."

Bridge sighed, but he wasn't going to argue over five minutes. "Fine. Twenty-five."

Nicole smiled, happy she got her way, but she felt like maybe she left something on the table. "Should've started at ten." Bridge just looked over at her and shook his head. "Twenty-five minutes, then we're going in."

"Unless they leave before that."

"They won't."

"That intuition thing again?" Bridge asked.

"No. She's just gotta be tired of all that driving and wanna sit down for a few minutes."

Ten minutes rolled by with still no sign of Werther or the other man she met. Nicole was starting to get impatient.

"Can we just go in now?"

"We agreed on twenty-five minutes," Bridge answered.

"But that was before."

"Before what?"

"Before I got tired of waiting."

"Fifteen more minutes."

Nicole sighed. "Let's just go in and get this over with."

"Patience."

"We've been in this car for an hour and a half."

"Legs cramping up?"

"I don't like sitting and waiting."

"I know."

"So can we?"

"Sure. In fifteen minutes."

"You're impossible. How did I ever fall in love with you?"

Bridge smiled. "You just couldn't help yourself."

Nicole raised an eyebrow. "True." She happened to glance at the backseat and thought of how they could pass the time while they were waiting. She put her hand on his arm and leaned over, kissing him on the cheek. "Hey, Luke."

"Yeah?"

"I have an idea how we could pass the time for the next few minutes."

Luke casually looked at her, then did a double-take, seeing the sultry look on her face. He knew what she wanted. "No, no!"

She retreated back to her seat. "Why not?"

"'Cause we're on an assignment here!"

"Nothing's happening."

"Yet!"

"What's the worst that could happen?"

"We could be back there doing the hanky-panky, and they leave us behind while we're still getting our pants on!"

"OK, so what's the next worst thing that could happen?"

"No! No! I give in to you a lot of times, but I'm putting my foot down here!"

Nicole loudly sighed to voice her displeasure. "Why do you have to be so formal all the time?"

"It's called doing our job?"

"We can still do our job and have a little fun at the same time."

Bridge rolled his eyes. "No. Not now. I'm putting my foot down."

"You can put your foot down back there."

As they continued debating the merits of having some extracurricular fun while they waited, Bridge's eyes were drawn to another vehicle that pulled up in front of the house.

"Wait, we got action."

"I wish we had action," Nicole said.

"No, stop. I mean it. Another car just pulled up."

Nicole sat up straight in her seat and looked at the car that Bridge pointed to. The car sat there for a few minutes, nobody getting out, nobody getting in, though the engine had turned off.

"Maybe they called an Uber," Nicole said.

Bridge looked on closely. "I kind of doubt it."

It was close to three minutes before there was any sign of life from the car. Finally, the driver's side door opened, revealing the driver. Nicole looked at her partner.

"What do we have here?"

Bridge stared at the driver as he walked to the house. "Bad news."

11

_____

Bridge and Nicole stared at the man as he entered the house and disappeared from sight.

"Isn't that um..."

Bridge nodded. "Greg Kenny."

"Well, I'd say this puts a wrap on it."

"On what?"

"We can now connect Kenny to Werther, and Werther to the car, and the car to us. That pretty much makes it a slam dunk that he was the one," Nicole said.

"Maybe it was the other guy in the house."

"Really?"

"Until we can positively put someone in that car, we have to keep all options open."

"At this point, I don't really care who was in the car. Let's just take these clowns out."

Bridge sighed, not liking what they might be running into. There was no telling how many more people were in that house. Could have been ten. Might have been zero. And he knew how dangerous Kenny was. So it was logical that whoever he had picked to associate with, that they were probably equally as dangerous.

"So how you wanna do this?" Nicole asked.

"I don't."

"Well, we've gotta do something, Luke. We can't just sit here."

"I don't wanna rush into something that we're not prepared for."

"If they come out of that house and go in separate cars, what do we do? Who do we follow?"

"We stay on Kenny. He's the number one target in all of this."

"I don't think we can afford to wait and let them get to their cars. Once that happens, who knows if we'll ever get this close to them again. Once they get in traffic, we can't guarantee we'll keep up with them."

Bridge rubbed his forehead. "I know." She was right. They couldn't let them get to their cars. But he wasn't very eager to walk into a situation where he didn't have all the facts. He pulled out his phone.

"What are you doing?"

"Calling Eric. I'm gonna see if he can get a team down here."

"What if they can't get here in time?"

"Then we'll have to improvise."

The phone rang, with Happ immediately picking up. "Yeah?"

"Eric, you busy right now?"

"Luke, I'm always busy. I assume you need something?"

"Yeah, you could say that," Bridge said. "I've got my eyes on a house right now that has Greg Kenny, Marianne Werther, and some other guy inside."

"You serious?"

"Deadly."

"Right this very second?"

"Yep."

"You're sure it's them?"

"Positive. We just had a conversation with Werther, followed her here, then we saw Kenny show up. Are you able to get a team down here? I'm not sure how many other than them are in here, and I'm not so keen on finding out alone."

"You don't do this when you're overseas, do you?"

"When I'm overseas, you're not available. You want in on this or not?"

"Yeah, yeah, we'll be on the way. Where you at?" Bridge gave him the address. "OK. We'll be there in twenty minutes."

"OK. If they start moving before that, I'll have to improvise."

"How you gonna do that?"

"I don't know. I'll figure something out."

"I'm sure you will. Twenty minutes. Just hold on."

"I'm holding."

Bridge put down the phone and took a deep breath, putting his eyes back on the house.

"Why'd you call Eric instead of the agency?" Nicole asked.

"Because they are not legally allowed to operate here. And if something goes down, if something goes awry, then it's gonna be an even bigger mess to clean up."

"Makes sense."

"Besides, if we can nab Kenny here, then I'll call P-One and let him know the FBI's got him. Then they can do their bargaining thing to figure out who gets him."

"Who do you think would get him?"

"Well, unless the FBI can prove he committed a crime here, which I have my doubts about, I'd imagine he'd be sent back to the agency."

"That he committed a crime or that they can prove it?"

"Either."

"And then the agency would drop him in a hole?"

"That's the idea."

"You think he's the mole? The one that Abbott was talking about?"

"I'd say that the odds are good," Bridge said. "It certainly looks that way. He quits, Abbott winds up dead, the PI who starts looking into it winds up dead, a car outside the PI's house starts shooting at us, the

CIA's involved, the car belongs to some woman who excels at lying, and that woman winds up at a house that Kenny also shows up at. That's an awful lot of coincidences if he's not involved. And you know how I feel about that."

"Maybe he's trying to find out what happened too?"

"Unlikely. He wouldn't have to quit and disappear to do that."

As they talked, the two of them put on their bullet-proof vests in case the action came sooner than anticipated.

"Who's this other guy that's in there?" Nicole asked. "Where do you think he fits in?"

"I don't know. Unless it's Stash."

"You really think so?"

"I don't really think anything at the moment. I'm just saying that nobody's ever seen the guy, and since we don't know who this is, maybe it fits." Bridge shrugged. "Maybe it doesn't fit. I don't know."

"By the way, you talk to Abbott?"

"Not today, why?"

"Just wondering how he was holding up. Gotta be tough having all this thrown in his face. Thinking he knows his brother and then finds out about all this other stuff. I imagine it's rough."

"Yeah. Just goes to show you, though. You never really know anybody unless you're living with them, and even then it's iffy."

"Guess that's true. You know, thinking about Kenny now, it's gonna be tough to take him alive."

"Men like him don't get taken alive," Bridge said. "They know what that means. Death is a much more satisfying proposition than being taken, thrown into a dark hole, beaten, and questioned. If he's got any type of choice to make, he'll go down with the ship."

"Well, let's hope we can stop that before he sinks."

Bridge looked at the time. "Twenty minutes is a long time to wait on this."

"It'll be fine."

As soon as the words left her lips, the front door to the house opened. The man they didn't recognize walked out, a couple of bags in each hand, plus a backpack on his shoulder.

"That doesn't look good," Nicole said.

"No, it doesn't. Looks like they're about to get out of here."

"What do you wanna do?"

Bridge quickly thought of a solution. "As soon as he gets back in the house, we rush it."

"Sounds good to me."

It wasn't much of a plan. But it didn't have to be. They only had to keep the people busy long enough to allow enough time for the FBI to get there. Bridge hoped they would be able to do that. Most shootouts and confrontations like this did not last that long. Maybe a few minutes at most, depending on the situation. And they had to keep them busy for at least fifteen. It was going to be a tall order. But they had to do it. There was no other choice. And they couldn't let the group escape. With their histories, and the way Kenny was able to blend in and disappear, they might not get another shot at him that was this good.

Bridge put his hand on the door and opened it slightly, just waiting for the other man to get back inside so he could jump out. As they waited, Nicole wondered about the engagement rules.

"What are we doing when we get there?"

"Talk first," Bridge replied.

"Why is that a thing?"

"What thing?"

"Why do we always talk first and give the bad guys the opportunity to shoot at us first?"

"Because that's the rules."

"There are no rules. Why can't we shoot first? We know they're gonna shoot at us, anyway. So why do we always give them the first shot? That doesn't seem fair."

Bridge shrugged. "Because we're good and they're not?"

"Seems so counterproductive."

"Maybe. But I think it's in the *Good Guy Handbook*."

"You're making stuff up."

"No, it's there. Chapter four, section six, paragraph three, subsection fourteen."

"Uh huh."

They watched as the man finished putting the bags in his car and walked back to the house. He closed the door once he was inside. That was their cue. Bridge and Nicole bolted out of their cars, guns drawn, and started running for the house. Unfortunately, their plan didn't work. They were about halfway there when the door opened again, the same guy walking out, having a few more bags in his hands. He immediately looked to his left and saw two people running his way. Considering they had guns and bulletproof vests, they didn't look like the kind of people he wanted to wait for.

"Cops!" the man yelled, ducking back inside and closing the door.

"Crap!" Bridge said. "There goes the element of surprise."

As they ran closer to the building, a few of the windows opened with guns sticking out of them. The flying bullets came next. Bridge and Nicole immediately ran for cover behind a car.

"There goes that idea," Nicole said.

Bridge looked at the time. "We just gotta keep them busy for a few minutes."

"Why don't you stand up and let them use you as a pinata? They can use you for target practice."

Bridge gave her a glance, but didn't respond. He took a deep sigh as he figured out what to do next. "We gotta get closer."

"I'm sure there's a back door, too. If we wait too long to move, they're gonna jet out the back."

"But their cars are out here. They'd have to go on foot."

"I think they'd take their chances over staying here in a shootout."

"Maybe."

"If we stay here, we're gonna lose them. The one guy yelled cops, so if they think we're feds or something, they're not gonna wait for the rest of the crew to show up. They know they wouldn't make it out."

Bridge sighed again. "I know. Damn." He didn't want it to go down this way.

The gunfire stopped for a few seconds, until Nicole poked her head above the car. "Well, looks like they're still there. For now."

"Fine. You try to keep them occupied, and I'll sneak around from the side."

"You got it."

It was going to take Bridge a little longer to get there as he scurried behind a bunch of cars parked along the street. He was going to go down to the next few houses, then come back up to the house from the side, so Kenny and company didn't have the same good view to shoot at him. Nicole jumped up and fired a few rounds at the window, then immediately ducked back down behind the car.

It took Bridge a few minutes to work his way around to the side of the house, but he finally managed it without incident. Remembering what Nicole had said about people ducking out the back, he made his way to the back door. Just as he got there, it started to open. He recognized Werther. He pointed his gun at her.

"Stop right there." Werther had one hand on the door, as she hadn't quite closed it yet, and the other hand on a bag. "Put your hands up, then lay down on the ground. Face first."

"You followed me here, didn't you?"

"Doesn't matter."

"And I thought I was being so careful. I was so sure I wasn't followed."

"Guess you were wrong," Bridge said. "Now, on the ground. Who else is in there?"

Werther acted like she was going to comply with his wishes and tossed her bag down on the ground. As she did, though, she took her hand off the door and put it on her side, where she removed a pistol and fired at Bridge. Bridge leaned to his right just as she got a shot off, hitting him in the vest and knocking him to the ground. She then retreated back inside. Though he was hit, the vest caught the bullet, and Bridge rolled around for a moment. It stung a little, but he would be OK.

Nicole heard the gunfire from the back of the house. "Luke, you OK back there?" Bridge just groaned into the mic. Nicole was getting worried. "Luke?"

Bridge took a couple breaths. His voice didn't sound the same. "I'm OK. Took one to the vest, but it didn't go through."

"You're sure you're OK?"

"Yeah. Just knocked the wind out of me, that's all."

"If we have to let them go, then we'll let them go."

"No. I'm good. How you making out?"

"I'm still busy."

"You were right," Bridge said, getting to his knees and then finding a nearby bush, not that it was great cover. "They're getting ready to leave."

"I don't know if we can hold them off, especially split up like we are."

Bridge looked at the door, thinking about making a run for it. Suddenly, all the gunfire had stopped.

"Luke, I don't like how quiet it suddenly got."

"Me neither. I get the feeling they're planning something."

"They might all bolt out the same door and take their chances."

"Could be."

"We still got a while before Eric gets here."

Bridge made a run for the back of the house, standing by the corner of it, out of sight if they came buzzing out the back door. Then, the door opened up, with Werther and Kenny slowly coming out, their guns raised and ready to shoot, looking for Bridge. As soon as they had their backs fully turned to Bridge, he appeared.

"Put 'em down," Bridge said. Kenny made a swift motion to turn around and start firing, but Bridge quickly put a stop to that. "Ah ah, I wouldn't do it. You'll never make it."

The two of them dropped their guns. Kenny turned around slowly, with Werther also doing the same. As Kenny looked at his adversary, there was something familiar about him.

"I know you from somewhere."

"We crossed paths once or twice before," Bridge said.

Kenny squinted his eyes as he tried to remember the face. Then he got it. "You were with the agency."

"I think it was the Ukraine when we last saw each other."

Kenny nodded. "Yeah. That was it. You got out soon after that as I recall."

"Yeah. Now I freelance. Work for myself."

"It was a good move."

It was almost like the two of them forgot the situation. They were talking like old friends that hadn't seen each other in a while. Like they didn't even realize there were guns being pointed, or that they had just been shooting at each other.

"Were you the mole? Is that why Gary Abbott died?"

"You shouldn't have gotten involved in this," Kenny answered. "Doesn't concern you."

"You the one who shot at me outside Bevell's place?"

A slight grin came over Kenny's face. "I wasn't

trying to kill you. I just wanted to give you a warning to back off."

"It didn't work."

"Clearly."

"What are you doing here?"

Kenny shrugged. "House-sitting."

Bridge smiled, then heard something alarming. It was a high-pitched kind of voice, coming from the house. He'd heard it before. It was that unmistakable voice he could never assume was anyone other than Chris Abbott. The sounds were faint, but he eventually made them out.

"Mr. Bridge!" The next one was still faint, but Bridge could hear it fine. "Luke!"

"Where is he?" Bridge asked.

Kenny shrugged. "Search me."

Bridge pointed to the house with his gun. "Show me. One false move and I'll shoot either one of you, clear?"

"Got it."

"Move."

Kenny and Werther slowly walked into the house, with Bridge right behind them. As soon as they walked into a room, Bridge stopped them.

"Where's Abbott and where's the other guy?"

"I'm right here," the other guy said, jumping out from the shadows and leveling Bridge with a right hand to the cheekbone.

Bridge stumbled back as Kenny jumped on top of

him. They started wrestling on the ground, each trying to get the upper hand. Nicole then broke through the front door, figuring something was going on since there was no gunfire. She ran into the room and immediately saw what was going on. She ran right into Werther, who was standing flatfooted, and not expecting what was coming. Nicole rammed her shoulder right into Werther's midsection, the force of the blow putting them both onto the floor, though Nicole wound up on top.

As Nicole straddled her opponent, she started throwing right and left hands alternatively, until the third man of the group rescued his partner. He grabbed Nicole by the arms and pulled her off. Nicole held her own against the man, surprising him with a few kicks. Werther got up and kicked at the back of Nicole's legs, bringing her to her knees. The man gave Nicole a back kick of his own, landing square on her jaw and knocking her over.

At this point, Bridge was getting the upper hand on Kenny. They were having a knockdown, drag out fight, with both getting in a ton of shots that would have put down a lesser man. By now, Bridge had Kenny on the ground and was delivering blow after blow. Kenny was just about out. Bridge's actions were interrupted, though, by the sound of Nicole's voice. It was a mix of a groan and a scream. But it was clear enough that she was in trouble. Bridge looked over at Nicole, seeing her get hoisted over the other man's head. Like he was a wrestler delivering a press slam, the man threw Nicole down. She landed hard on top of a coffee table, which stood up from the thump at first, then suddenly broke apart. Nicole lay there in a considerable amount of pain.

Bridge got up and charged at the man, ramming him in the stomach with his shoulder. Their momentum was stopped when the man's back hit the wall behind him. Bridge immediately started working the man over, and was clearly getting the upper hand, and not by a little. Seeing Nicole get thrown around like that flipped a switch inside him, making him look like an MMA fighter who was going in for the kill. There was nothing that was going to stop him from taking the man down and out. Except someone coming up behind him.

A few seconds later, Werther grabbed a weapon, which turned out to be Bridge's gun, and hit its owner in the back of the head with all of her might. Bridge went down. With Bridge laying there, seemingly out of commission, Werther ran over to Kenny to help him get back to his feet. The man that Bridge was just battling took a few seconds to get his breath back, but then came over to them as well.

"C'mon, we've gotta get out of here," Werther said.

"Let's finish them off first," the other man said.

"No," Kenny replied. "She's right. We don't have time for that. They've probably got help on the way already. We can't get stuck here and worry about anything else."

"Our bags are outside," Werther said.

Kenny pointed to the other man. "You get our bags from out back, then head out of here."

"Right."

The man left, and Kenny looked at Werther. "You're coming with me."

"What about my car?"

"It's compromised. Leave it."

They started to go out the front door when Werther suddenly stopped. "Wait, what about Abbott? We need him."

"Oh. Almost forgot about him. Get the car started. I'll bring him out."

Werther went to the car and waited, getting nervous about any help showing up. She kept looking at the rearview and side mirrors. She watched as the other man got in the car and took off. She then looked at the door and saw Kenny bringing Abbott out. As soon as he put their prisoner in the car, Werther thought she detected an unmarked SUV approaching.

"We gotta go! Now!"

Kenny jumped in the front seat, and Werther floored it, passing the unmarked FBI vehicle a few seconds later. She kept her eyes peeled on the mirrors for the next few minutes to make sure no one was following them. It appeared they just made it.

"Whew. That was close."

"Too close," Kenny said. "We got sloppy. We can't let that happen again."

"We won't."

"I hope not. Because if we get surprised by those two again... well, I would hate to have to kill them."

12

"Luke. Luke." Happ stood over Bridge's lifeless body. He turned his friend over and Bridge started twitching his arms. Happ then looked over at Nicole, who was holding the back of her head, which slammed into the table on her way down.

"I think she'll be OK," another agent said.

By now, Bridge had started moving his head around. His eyes were fluttering. Almost simultaneously, Bridge and Nicole began sitting up at the same time, each holding the back of their heads.

"Hold it now," Happ said. "Take it easy. Looks like you took one pretty good." Happ helped position Bridge so his back was up against the wall. "Just relax."

"Luke, you OK?" Nicole asked, crawling over to her boyfriend. Bridge put his arm around her.

Happ smiled and shook his head. "Now that's true

love. The couple that gets beaten up together, stays together."

"If I felt better, you know I'd have a comment for that," Bridge said.

"I know. I figure I should get my licks in now while you can't think of anything."

"Smart strategy."

"So what happened here? Other than you two getting your asses beat."

Bridge rolled his head around and grimaced. "They started leaving. So we had to try to keep them busy until you got here."

"Looks like you did that. Partially. Would've preferred if you didn't use yourself as human battering rams, though. Who was here? Other than Werther."

"Kenny. And another guy. Don't know his name."

"Just the three of them? That all?"

"Isn't that enough?"

"Turned out those three were plenty," Nicole said.

"So it seems," Happ replied. Bridge attempted to get up, but Happ used his muscle to keep his friend seated. "Just sit tight. We got paramedics on the way to check you guys out first."

"I'm fine," Bridge said.

"OK, well, as soon as the paramedics say that and clear you, then you can get out."

"It's not the first time I've had my bell rung."

"Don't I know it? Even still, you're gonna sit and wait."

Bridge looked over at his girlfriend. "How you feeling?"

"Now I know how you felt. Getting thrown through a table is no fun."

"You guys can now compare injuries later," Happ said. "War stories of getting thrown around and rag-dolled and tossed into objects and breaking them." Bridge was going to reply, but the pain in his head prevented him from speaking. "So can you tell me what happened exactly?"

"Which part?"

"Well, I guess you can skip the part where you guys get the crap beaten out of you." Happ faked a smile. "I already saw that part."

"Well, like I said, we were just trying to keep them busy until you got here. They started putting bags in a car, so we figured they were about to rabbit."

"We started to approach the house," Nicole said. "Then they started shooting."

"So I made my way to the back of it, and finally two of them, Kenny and Werther, came out the back. I got the jump on them. Then I heard a voice." Bridge turned his head sharply toward Nicole. "Did you hear Chris' voice?"

"Abbott?"

"Yeah."

Nicole shook her head, though slowly. "No, I didn't hear it. It was him?"

"Definitely. That's a voice I wouldn't mistake anywhere."

"You're sure it was Chris Abbott?" Happ asked.

"No question. Like I said, he's got an unmistakable voice. I'd know it anywhere."

"Haven't had the pleasure of hearing it."

"It's a higher-pitched voice. You'd never mistake it for someone else."

Nicole put her hand on Bridge's arm. "Wait, if they have him..."

Happ turned to another of the agents there. "Hey, try to run down Chris Abbott. Might have a kidnapping."

A few minutes later, the paramedics arrived, and they started working on Nicole and Bridge. After they were done, Happ asked for the damage report.

"What's the verdict?"

The female paramedic spoke up. "They both took a good shot. It's possible they have concussions, but I can't be sure. They'd have to get checked out at the hospital to know for sure."

"I'm not going anywhere," Bridge said.

"He probably has one. She might not. They both got walloped pretty good. They're actually lucky it's not worse. He's got a slight cut on the back of his head, but it's not too bad. Won't need stitches or anything."

Bridge opened his eyes wide. "I'm fine. I don't have a concussion."

"How do you know?" Happ asked.

Bridge flicked his eyes and looked at the light. "See? Light doesn't bother me at all." He put two fingers in front of his face. "Look, two fingers. No blurry vision, light doesn't bother me, everything's good."

"You're not gonna go, are you?"

"Nope." Bridge slowly got back to his feet.

"Luke..."

"Eric..."

"Nicole..."

"Luke..."

Happ just looked at the two of them and shook his head. "It's like a Three Stooges routine."

"Well, there are three of us here," Bridge said.

"Uh, yeah. Anyway..."

"Ain't got time for the hospital. Abbott's out there and who knows what they want him for. If we don't find him soon, alive, we'll be finding him dead."

"Well, one thing's for sure, they're gonna be in the city somewhere."

"What makes you so sure?" Nicole asked.

"Where else could they go? We'll put alerts out on all the planes, trains, subways, buses, and boats. They'll have to hole up somewhere again."

"Don't be so sure," Bridge said.

"Why?"

"Because you're dealing with Greg Kenny. He's a master at disguising himself. He can blend into anything he wants to. That's the life he's used to. He doesn't have to put himself out there in the open. He can become whatever he wants to be."

"Still, we'll have alerts out. He's not going anywhere. Plus, he's got the other two with him, right?"

"If I had to guess, I'd say they're probably equally as capable of doing the same. Kenny wouldn't associate himself with a bunch of idiots."

As they stood there talking, Bridge started zoning out. But it wasn't from the effects of his head getting crushed. He was already contemplating his next steps.

"You all right?" Nicole asked.

"Yeah. I was just thinking..."

"You're not supposed to do that," Happ quipped.

"Yeah, yeah. I have a feeling that Werther isn't who she appears to be."

"We kind of already know that," Nicole said.

"No, I mean, I have a feeling that Werther is an alias. I bet she has a different name elsewhere."

"Possible."

"And I'm willing to bet that if we were to look at some pictures of people that Kenny's associated with, we might find out who that other guy is too."

"It's gonna take me a while to come up with that."

"I wasn't talking about you. There's someone else who's already got all that on file."

Nicole raised her eyebrows. "You're talking about..."

"I am. Things will go a lot faster. And we don't have time to waste here."

As the FBI covered the scene, Bridge and Nicole gingerly got back to their feet, taking a few more minutes for the pain to lessen. They each took a few steps, while staying in the same general location, making sure they were good enough to continue.

"You all right?" Happ asked.

Bridge nodded and felt the back of his head. "Yeah. It'll take more than that to take me out of commission."

"You're lucky they didn't kill you. Both of you. They had the chance to."

"They were probably in too much of a hurry to get out of here to wanna worry about us."

"They had to assume we were coming soon. Lucky for you."

"Yeah. This might be one of the few times you can get the crap kicked out of you and feel like you're the lucky one."

"It was my fault," Nicole said. "Luke was winning his fight."

"We were outnumbered. We did what we could. One on one, I'd take our chances all day long. Both of us."

As Nicole kept talking to Happ, Bridge stepped outside, not wanting anyone else to hear his conversation. He dialed a familiar number.

"Yes?"

"This is Alpha One-Two-Seven-Six-Five."

"OK?"

"I need to speak to Pinnacle One. Now."

"I'm not sure that is feasible at the moment."

"Tell him it's urgent. I need him... now."

"Stand by."

As a few FBI agents came near him, Bridge wandered even farther away from the house, getting closer to the street to avoid any listening ears. It was a good three or four minutes before Pinnacle One got on the phone.

"Luke, what's the emergency?"

"I just ran into our friend Greg Kenny."

Pinnacle One hesitated for a second. "So he is here."

"Yes. And he's got friends, apparently."

"What happened?"

"Got a lead on a woman," Bridge said. "Met her, she lied to my face, then we followed her to a house, where she met Kenny and another guy I haven't identified."

"They got away?"

"Temporarily. I tried to do what I could, but they outnumbered and overpowered us."

"I see."

"There's something else. They also had Chris Abbott as a hostage."

"Gary's brother?"

"Yeah. Now what would they be doing with him?"

"I don't know."

"Is he somehow involved with you as well?"

"No. I swear to you he's got no involvement with us."

"Well, Kenny's got him for a reason. Just have to figure out what it is."

"Where do you think he's going?"

"I don't know yet," Bridge answered. "I was hoping I could come in, look at some of your files, put some names to the faces." Pinnacle One was silent for a few seconds. Bridge knew he was hesitant to allow any unauthorized personnel into the building. "Listen, if you wanna find this guy, and quickly, you need to help me as much as you can. I can do some of this on my own, but it's gonna take longer. If I can look at some of the people that Kenny's known to be involved with, maybe I can make them out, and we can piece together where he plans on going."

"Fine. How soon can you get here?"

"Half hour?"

"I'll have someone waiting for you in the lobby."

"Good. Thank you."

After hanging up, Bridge looked down the street and sighed. He then held his head. "What is all this about?" he said to himself.

Bridge headed back inside. He found Nicole and Happ standing next to each other, still talking. He tugged on her arm.

"We gotta go."

"Wait, where are you going?" Happ asked.

"We have to see a former... associate."

"Let me in."

Bridge shook his head. "Sorry, bud, can't. It's not up

to me. Just us going into the building is against protocol. It's only supposed to be active agency employees who are working on that project."

"What's the project's name?"

Bridge grinned. "Can't say."

"Where's this building located?"

Bridge's grin got even bigger. "Can't say."

"What can you say?"

"That I can't say."

"Well, do you think you'll be able to loop me in when you're done?"

"I would think so. We'll see. Depends on how classified the information is."

Happ sighed. "I have a feeling you're gonna freeze me out."

"I won't. I'll tell you everything I can. You know how it works with secret government agencies."

"No, I don't know. How is it?"

Bridge smiled again. "Can't say."

"Are you gonna say anything?"

Bridge shrugged. "See you later?"

"Gee, thanks. You get this place shot to pieces and then hightail it somewhere else and leave me with the cleanup."

"At least there's no bodies."

"Yeah. Thanks."

Bridge tapped his friend on the arm. "The least I could do."

"The very least."

"You sure you wanna go back there?" Nicole asked.

Bridge shrugged. "Why not? I don't have any unpleasant memories."

"Maybe it'll make you wanna sign back up again."

Bridge laughed. "Nothing could make me wanna do that again. Too dangerous."

"Yeah, like what we do now is so safe."

13

It was familiar, but different. The layout was pretty much the same as the last time Bridge had been in there. There was a receptionist's desk in the middle of the lobby, but not much else. It'd gone through an upgrade in its design, though. Everything looked brand new. And expensive. Alternating marble-colored tiles on the floor and stone tiles on the wall. It was a ten-floor office building. At least that's how it appeared on the outside. Bridge and Nicole immediately looked at their surroundings as they walked in.

"Can I help you?" the receptionist asked.

"Yeah, I am expected," Bridge said

"Your name?"

"Luke Bridge. This is my assistant, Nicole."

The receptionist immediately got on the phone to let someone know of the visitors. Bridge and Nicole stood there until someone came down for them. They crossed their arms and discussed the building.

"Nice place," Nicole said.

"Believe me, it didn't look this inviting when I worked here."

Nicole looked around. "You ever wonder about places like these?"

"What do you mean?"

"Look around. A high-level CIA building here in New York and anyone can waltz through those doors. No guards on the stairway, an elevator right past a receptionist who probably couldn't stop anybody, and front doors that aren't locked or guarded or anything."

Bridge smiled. "You can tell you spent all your time at Langley."

"Why's that?"

"What's the number one rule if you wanna blend in somewhere?"

Nicole shrugged. "I dunno. Act like you belong there?"

Bridge nodded. "So if you have a top-secret field office somewhere, that you don't want anyone to know about, what would you do?"

"Act like it's not a field office."

"There you go."

"But I mean... anyone can walk right in here."

"Not really. For one, nobody's going to walk in here that doesn't have business here. And just by chance, if someone does happen to stumble in here, or an enemy or something, they're not going anywhere."

Nicole pointed to the stairs. "Uh..."

"Yeah. If someone were to blow in here and run past her and go up those steps, there'll be some gates that close, preventing them from coming down, effectively trapping them in."

"If they get to another floor?"

"All the doors are sealed close. They have a scanner attached. They only open if you scan your ID badge."

"I'm assuming the elevator works in a similar fashion?"

"You can hit those little numbered buttons until you're blue in the face, those doors are not opening unless you scan your ID badge first."

"So you're basically locked out of going anywhere unless you've got a badge?"

"Pretty much."

"So if I ever wanna break in here, I should probably follow someone home, steal their badge, then break back in?"

Bridge leaned in and whispered to her. "You do realize they can probably hear everything we're saying right now, right?"

"Oh."

Bridge smiled. "It is a CIA building after all. Hidden and concealed mics everywhere."

"Right. Just kidding about that stealing the badge part. And breaking in. And the rest of it."

About ten seconds later, the elevator door opened. A younger man, probably in his mid-to-late twenties, stepped off. Bridge knew the type. He was probably the designated gopher who had to greet all visitors who came in and take them to their designated location. He walked up to Bridge and shook his hand.

"Luke Bridge?"

"That's me."

"Follow me."

As Bridge and Nicole started walking to the elevator, the man stopped and turned around. He looked at Nicole.

"I'm sorry, I was told to only expect one of you."

"She's with me," Bridge said.

"Only authorized people are allowed to go up."

"I authorized her."

"My instructions were to bring you."

"She goes where I go."

"I'm sorry, but—"

"Listen, she's also a former agent who's had a top-level security clearance. There's nothing up there that she hasn't seen before."

"My instructions were still—"

"Listen, I don't care what your instructions were. We either go up together, or I walk out of here right now. And I don't think your boss will like that."

"Just a moment."

The man went over to the desk and grabbed the phone to make a call.

"Thanks for standing up for me," Nicole said.

"Always. It's not really his fault. He's just trying to do what he's told and not make a wrong step."

"I get it."

The man put the phone down and walked back over to them. "Both of you follow me."

Bridge kept a stoic look on his face, not wanting to show the man up by having a cocky grin on his face for being right. They went over to the elevator, the man scanning his badge, then hitting the button for the tenth floor. They stepped inside.

"Oh, getting the grand tour, huh?" Bridge asked. Nicole looked at him, wondering what he meant. "Usually in these buildings, the higher the floor, the more important the people."

Nicole looked at the corners of the elevator. There was something unusual about them. They had small grates in all the corners. She tapped Bridge on the arm and pointed them out.

"Oh," Bridge said, recognizing it immediately. "They're for extreme security breaches. If someone did have a fake badge and got on here, there's hidden cameras embedded in the walls, and the elevator is monitored. So someone would manually lock the doors to prevent them from opening on any floor. Then some type of toxic gas would be unleashed and kill whoever was in here. Or knock them out so they can be questioned later." Bridge then leaned forward to talk to the other man. "Which one are they doing these days?"

The man looked a little annoyed to even talk about it. "I really can't say."

Bridge took a step back, looked at Nicole, and shrugged.

"What are the other floors for?" Nicole asked.

"Each one has a specific task. Top floor was usually offices for the top brass, as well as a situation room, and the analysts' station. That way if something went down, the top guys just had to go down the hall instead of going up and down floors. The other floors are usually support roles. IT, Psych, interview rooms, things like that."

"Seems a lot more intricate than what I worked at. Not as much cloak and dagger where I was."

"Well, to be fair, where you were, everyone was already aware of what that building was. This is secret."

"True."

Just as they got to the tenth floor, and the doors opened, the man turned back to his guests. "Remember the protocols as a visitor."

"I got it," Bridge said with a grin. "Don't make any sudden turns, go in any rooms I'm not invited into, don't make notes about what's going on, and definitely don't remember anything I see on any screens. I've worked here before. I think I know the drill."

"Follow me."

"Well, you are leading the way."

They stepped off the elevator and walked down a short hallway, with several doors on each side, all of them closed. They came to the end of the hall, which then split left and right into longer hallways. They went right. They were soon greeted with glass doors, which needed an ID badge to get through. There were a few more doors, also closed, and then another glass door, badge also required.

"You sure this is an office or a maze?" Nicole asked.

"Maybe a bit of both," Bridge replied.

They took another turn, left this time, and walked past a huge room with glass windows. They saw a bunch of people sitting at desks this time, with monitors on the wall. Bridge looked over at Nicole and whispered.

"Situation room."

They continued walking down the hall until they got to an office. The door was also closed.

"Wait here." Their host knocked on the door and went inside.

"This has been fun," Nicole said.

Bridge put his hands in the pockets of his pants. "Yeah. A real blast."

"Like old home week for you. Miss it?"

Bridge looked around for a few seconds, then shook his head. "No. Not at all. All this cloak-and-dagger stuff, it gets to you after a while."

"Can't say what we do now is a whole lot different."

"Sure it is. Some of the jobs may be similar, but the way we operate isn't."

"Maybe we should move our operations out of your hotel and find a place like this."

"Our hotel."

"Your hotel. I want a house, remember?"

"Oh. Yeah. Anyway, too many doors to walk through here."

"Yeah, I imagine it gets annoying after a while."

"How many doors did you have to walk through where you were?"

"Uh, two I think."

"Not too bad."

"I guess. Do you think when we go in there we can call him by his actual name now, or do we still have to deal with all the technical code name nonsense?"

"Does it matter?"

Nicole shrugged. "I guess not. Just seems kind of silly to call someone Pinnacle One to his face instead of his actual name."

"Then call him by his name, I don't care."

A few seconds later, the door opened, and the man stood there, waving his guests inside. After they were inside, the man closed the door. Almost immediately, Pinnacle One was greeting them. He shook each of their hands.

"Thanks for coming."

Nicole smiled at him. "Thank you, Mr... uh... One."

He laughed. "In here you can call me Joe. Enough of that technical code name nonsense."

Nicole looked at her boyfriend and smiled. "I like this guy."

"I hope bringing her doesn't cause a problem," Bridge said.

Joe looked at Nicole and smiled. "Not at all. She's ex-agency anyway, right? Nothing she hasn't seen before. Besides, she brightens up the building." He then walked past his guests and went out the door, everyone else following him. "We're just gonna go down the hall here to another room where we have some people working."

"That main room with the glass?" Nicole asked.

"No, that's for major active situations that require all hands on deck. We're just gonna go to a slightly smaller room. No windows."

"Oh."

They did go to a smaller room, but it wasn't that much smaller. It just seemed more closed off since there were no windows. But there were around a dozen people working at their computer stations. And there were still plenty of monitors on the walls.

"Since we spoke, Luke, I already had these guys starting to work on things."

"Good," Bridge replied. "Come up with anything yet?"

Joe went over to a desk and tapped one of the analysts on the back. "Pull up all of Kenny's known associates." The analyst nodded and brought up a bunch of pictures within seconds. Joe then looked at Bridge. "Any of these guys look like your mysterious friend at the house with Kenny?"

Bridge noticed an empty chair by the analyst. "May I?"

The analyst pointed to it and moved his over a little. "Sure. Be my guest."

There were pictures of six guys on the monitor, taking over the entire size of the screen. "None of these guys."

"Just use the mouse to scroll down for more, and it'll bring a new setup."

Bridge scrolled through a few more sets of pictures, not finding anyone that looked familiar. He was mostly paying attention to the face. Hair color and style could change easily and often did when dealing with people who were good at disappearing. He was about halfway through the pictures when one guy stood out to him.

"Wait, that looks like him." Bridge pointed to the top right picture on the screen. He looked back at Nicole. "What do you think?"

Nicole leaned forward. She nodded. "That's him."

Joe looked at the both of them. "You're sure?"

"Positive. He picked me up and threw me through a table. I wouldn't forget his face."

"A table?"

"Yeah."

Joe looked her up and down. "And you're still standing?"

"I always get back up."

Joe was impressed with her toughness. "You sure you wouldn't like to get back into the agency?"

Nicole smiled. "Thanks. But I got a job."

"I might be able to pay more."

"Thanks, but money's not the only payment I like or get."

Joe raised his eyebrows and cleared his throat. Bridge closed his eyes and tried to remain emotionless. Joe sidestepped the remarks and focused back to her skills. "I remember reading your file, but I don't recall you ever being in the field."

"Nope. Just an analyst."

"No field work?"

Nicole shook her head. "Not until I met this guy."

"Remarkable. I think the agency missed its calling with you."

"Guess it's too late now."

"If this guy ever terminates your employment, you come and see me, all right? There'd always be a position open here for you."

"Thanks. I'll keep that in mind."

Bridge hung his head. Just what he needed. Another thing she could hold over his head to get her way. "Can we get back to discussing our guy here?"

"Oh, yeah," Joe said. "Who is he?"

The analyst stepped back in and clicked on the

picture. All the other pictures faded away, and the picture of Steele Magareth moved to the side. The other side of the screen was devoted to his information.

"Steele Magareth," the analyst said, "was one of Greg Kenny's confidants in Europe when he was there."

"Agency?" Joe asked.

"No. Looks like he once belonged to a rebel/terrorist group in Ukraine."

They read off Magareth's qualifications and skills. After they were done, Joe looked at Nicole.

"Looks like you got off easy getting thrown through that table."

"Tell me about it," Nicole replied.

"What about the other one?" Bridge asked. "Marianne Werther. I'll be surprised if that's her real name."

"I already did some checking on her," the analyst said. He brought up Werther's picture and profile.

"That's her. That's our little angel."

"If she's an angel, then god help all of us," Joe said.

"What's her story?" Nicole asked.

"Turns out, surprise, surprise, that's not her real name," the analyst said. "Her real name is actually Zara Dalton."

"Ring any bells with anybody?" Bridge asked.

"Well, turns out, she's a former MI6 agent."

"Former?"

"Yes. She left MI6 over a year ago."

"Roughly the same time that Kenny left," Joe said.

"What's also interesting is when I last checked Magareth's movements," the analyst said. "The last confirmed location I got on him was also about a year ago."

"Where was that?" Bridge asked.

"Serbia."

"A hotbed for illegal weapons," Joe said. "So now you're telling me that we have an ex-CIA agent, ex-MI6 agent, and a terrorist or whatever he is, all aligned with each other and probably have been for the last year?"

"Well, I mean, it kind of looks that way."

"What do we have on this Dalton?"

"Not much, really. Good record. Left on good terms, presumably, from what I see."

"What's behind the curtain doesn't always match what's on the outside."

Another analyst shouted from the other side of the room. "Sir, Greg Kenny's name just popped up at the airport."

"What? Are you kidding me?"

"Looks as though he just bought a ticket on the next plane to France."

"France? What the devil's he doing there?" Joe then looked to the younger man who escorted Bridge and Nicole in. "I want you to alert the FBI and inform them of what's going on. You need to tell them only what we need them to know."

"Yes, sir."

As the man left the room, Bridge leaned back in his seat, his arms crossed and his thumb pressed against his lips. He was deep in thought.

Nicole nudged him. "What are you thinking?"

"I think you can forget about the airport."

"Why's that?" Joe asked.

"I mean, Kenny's not stupid enough to use his name to try to fly out of here right now," Bridge said. "He knows you'd be watching. You can send the FBI there if you want to, but I guarantee he's not there."

"Diversion?"

Bridge nodded. "I would think so."

"For what? What's his play?"

"He wants to draw you in one direction so he can go in another."

"But which way?"

"If he wants to get out of the country, what's the best way to do it? Assuming he wants to do it discreetly."

"Mexico," Nicole said.

Bridge's eyes almost rolled out of his head. "Oh, don't say it. Please don't say it."

"Mexico."

"Ugh. Why do you have to torment me so?"

"That'd be my choice," Joe replied.

"He's got a long way to get there," Bridge said.

"I agree."

"So that means I gotta assume he's gonna know the

airport thing's a trick. He's also going to know we're gonna assume Mexico's his next play."

"So why would he do it then?" Nicole asked.

"He won't."

"But you just said..."

"I said that would be the next logical progression. That's why he won't do it. He'll get us chasing after him going five different ways, while he does nothing."

Nicole put her hands over her head. "My brain hurts."

"You think he's gonna wait?" Joe asked.

Bridge nodded. "I do."

"But why?"

"Too much heat. He knows he can't get out with all these eyes on him. He'll wait. Let things cool down. Then he'll get out nice and easy."

"What makes you think so?"

"Because that's what I would do."

"I don't understand what he needs Abbott for, though," Nicole said.

"Maybe he just plans on wiping out the entire family so there's no more inquiries," Joe said.

"I don't think so," Bridge said.

"Why not?"

"If he wanted Abbott dead, he could've done it back at that house. But he didn't. He chose to take him with him. That means he needs him for something."

"But what?" Nicole asked.

"I don't know. What... that's the question."

14

It'd been five days since the encounter at the house. Since then, there'd been very little action regarding anything by anybody. Bridge was working the phone all day, trying to get some type of lead. So far, nothing had materialized. He called Joe to see if his people had come up with anything, but they hadn't. He called Happ to see if he had heard anything, but he hadn't either. Everything was quiet. Too quiet for Bridge's liking. But there wasn't much else he could do except continue to plug along and hope for the best. After getting off the phone and letting out a loud sigh, he rejoined Nicole in the living room. She could hear his frustration.

"I take it the news is the same as the last few days?"

"Yeah," Bridge replied. "None."

"Well, I guess we can take it as a small positive."

"Yeah? Why's that?"

"At least it means that Abbott's not dead yet."

"Yet. Yet is the operative word there. If we don't find him soon, I'm sure that won't hold up forever. Unless he's the surprise ring leader, as soon as they're done with whatever they need him for, they'll dump him."

"You don't suppose, do you?"

"Suppose what?"

"That this has all been orchestrated... by him?"

"Who?"

"Abbott?"

"You mean he's actually in charge of this mess?"

Nicole shrugged. "Just a thought."

"Now that'd be all kinds of messed up."

"Wouldn't be the first time."

"Nah, I can't see it. Can you?"

"No, not really. I just thought I'd throw it out there."

"I mean, what would be the point of drawing us in?" Bridge asked.

"I agree."

"If he was in charge, he'd have had an easier time of it if we weren't involved, so, no, I can't see him pulling the strings on this."

"I agree. Just a thought."

"Question is, what do they need him for?"

"We've been pondering that question for days, Luke."

"And we've still got no answers."

Bridge sat down and started thinking, trying to figure out what Kenny would want with Chris Abbott.

It was something that he needed him alive for. But what? They weren't involved in the same business, and Chris didn't have any idea what his brother was into as far as being mixed up with the CIA. So what would the connection be? Bridge went over to his computer and started going over all the information again. After a little while, he brought up pictures of the two brothers, putting them side by side on the screen. He stared at them for a few minutes before it finally hit him.

"That's it."

Nicole heard him saying something and looked over at him. "What?"

"That's it."

"What's it?"

"I think I know what they want him for."

Nicole came over to Bridge and looked at the screen. She didn't see it, though. "What?"

Bridge pointed at the two pictures. "Look. They look similar."

"Well, they are brothers, you know."

"I know. That's the point. They're brothers. They look similar."

"And?"

"And that's why they want him. They need someone who looks like Gary Abbott. Since that's obviously not possible, they need someone who looks just like him. Who would that be?"

"Chris Abbott," Nicole answered. "I mean, I get your logic, but I don't understand why. What would they need his face for? They didn't work together, so, I... I don't know what the point would be."

Bridge put his hand over his mouth as he leaned back in his chair and thought about it. He took a few deep breaths. "Here's a few possibilities."

"OK?"

"They need his face to access something. To pretend he's his brother so they can get something. Maybe money? Maybe something else, I don't know."

"Or?"

"Or maybe they will play it off like he's his brother and exchange him for something. A ransom, reward, debt, something like that."

"I don't think that'll stand up. With all of the ways you can identify people's identities these days, plus the fact that I'm sure Chris wouldn't just willfully go along with it, they wouldn't be able to fool anybody for more than a day at most."

"Which would bring us back to the other point. They need him, his face, his presence, something, to get something for them."

"But what? They obviously didn't know each other."

Bridge sat there staring at the screen. Then another thought hit them. What if they were going about this case the wrong way? Maybe they had the whole thing wrong from the get-go.

"What if they did?"

"What?" Nicole said. "If Abbott, Gary, was blowing the whistle on them, then..."

"What if he wasn't?"

"Huh?"

"What if it's all wrong? What if Kenny wasn't the mole Abbott was talking about?"

"I don't understand."

"Just a guess that I'm throwing out here, but what if Abbott was actually in business with Kenny somehow? Then Abbott throws out some mole story, that may or may not actually be true, getting the CIA to look more heavily into that, then whatever it was he and Kenny were doing."

"I dunno, Luke, we've looked at the records, the CIA's looked at the records, there's nothing to suggest the two knew each other. There's nothing to even suggest that Abbott was into anything nefarious."

"I know, I know. But we know Kenny's reputation. He's a master manipulator, can hide anything or anyone."

"But... and I say but... if that's the case, and they actually were in bed together, then why would he kill him? What sense would that make? And why wait a year to get his brother if that's what he needed him for?"

Bridge shook his head. "I don't know. I don't have any of those answers. I'm not even sure I have any of the right questions. It just seems like maybe that's a better theory than what we've been working with."

"It doesn't really make sense any which way you slice it. Either the way we've been thinking or now. I dunno. Maybe he doesn't really need Chris for anything. Maybe we just haven't found his body yet."

"No, I don't think so. If he was planning on killing him, he could've done it already. Back at the house, or even before the house, wherever it was that they took him from. They didn't need to take him with them. But they did. Why? 'Cause they need him for something. And the only reason I can think of, is that they need him to finish something that his brother started. And if that's the case, they must have been in cahoots."

"Maybe Kenny is just aware of something that Abbott was into."

"How would he know unless he was involved?"

"I don't know. I'm not liking this very much."

"Join the club."

Bridge was just about to call Pinnacle One with his theories when his phone suddenly rang. He was surprised to see it was the same number he was about to call.

"Joe, we must be reading each other's minds. I was just about to call you."

"Regarding the same thing, I take it?"

"I'm not sure. What are you calling for?"

"I'm calling about Kenny and company slipping out of the country."

"What?"

"I take it that's not what you had to say then?"

"No, it wasn't. What happened?"

"Not sure. We just found out a few hours ago."

"There goes my theory about waiting a while," Bridge said. "How'd they get out?"

"As far as we can tell, it happened two days ago. We've been backtracking their steps to figure out how they did it. They must have travelled down to North Carolina by car. They took a flight from there to Brazil. And then from Brazil to Paris."

"Smart. They avoided the obvious places we'd look. But their names still should have popped up somewhere."

"Would've if they used them. They had aliases and fake passports for everybody."

"Including Abbott?"

"That's affirmative."

"That would indicate that this has been in the works for a while. You can't just pick up a fake passport anywhere. And someone like Kenny would only use someone he can trust or knows well. That would tell me that he's on a schedule."

"Possibly."

"I've been thinking this past week that he took Abbott because of the pressure we were putting on him, but maybe that's not it at all. Maybe this is what he was planning all along. That's why he didn't wait a while before moving. He couldn't. It'd throw off his plan."

"Which we still don't know what that is."

"How'd you get wind of this?"

"Our partners at MI6 alerted us to them getting a hit on Magareth at the airport in France. They did some digging, wound up getting some pictures of him, Dalton, and Abbott all coming out of the airport together."

"Not Kenny?"

"Not in the picture, but you can be certain he was there. We've done some digging on the flight manifests, and there was a party of three that travelled from North Carolina, to Brazil, then to Paris."

"Magareth and company."

"Correct. We also found a solo passenger, male, who also took the same flights at the same times."

"Kenny."

"Also correct. We've traced that name to a seldom used alias that we believe is him."

"So they all used fake names. Any hits or connections to those?"

"We are currently running down all possible avenues in relation to that, but so far we haven't gotten anything."

"Probably won't either. I doubt they'd use names that we could trace back to them in another capacity."

"You're probably right about that."

"It was smart of them to split up like they did," Bridge said. "They know a party of four would come under scrutiny. And the usual split-up of two and two would cause an eyebrow to be raised too."

"Even if they stayed together, we wouldn't have found out about it until after they were gone anyway with the names that they used. They just went the extra mile for it."

"What's the connection to Paris, do you think?"

"We can't deduce that there is one. Right now, as it appears, it might have just been a convenient place to fly in to."

"Where'd they go since then?"

"Unknown. We haven't been able to pick them up since."

"Rental car?"

"Negative."

"Which means they had a car waiting," Bridge said. "And probably a fourth member of the team."

"Quite possibly. You said you were thinking about calling. What was your news?"

"Well, wasn't really news. Just kind of some theories that I've been kicking around."

"Might as well spill them. Can't be any worse than some of the ones we've been sitting on. Maybe you'll hit on something."

Bridge then told him everything that he'd come up with. As he talked about it, he became even more convinced that he may have been right. He had no proof of anything yet. But he had that nagging feeling deep in his gut that this went deeper than the current prevailing theory.

"Only one problem with that," Joe said.

"What's that?"

"We've already cross-referenced Gary Abbott and Kenny to see if their paths had crossed anywhere."

"I take it that they didn't?"

"They did not. At least not that we've dug up. We haven't found any evidence that they were ever in the same location at the same time."

"What about Magareth?"

"Well, we've connected him and Kenny to Ukraine, but nothing between him and Abbott either."

"What about Abbott and Dalton?" Bridge asked.

"You know, that's one we haven't checked on yet. Since we found out her identity the other day, we've been focused on finding her current location."

"Understandable. But if we found out where she's been, we might find out where she's going."

15

Bridge and Nicole were led to the elevator by the same man as the last time they'd been there.

"I could kind of get used to this," Nicole said.

"Don't."

"It's not so bad."

"I beg to differ," Bridge said.

Once off the elevator, they went to the same room as they'd been in before. Joe was already in there waiting for them. He shook each of their hands as they came in.

"Looks like we've learned some more information," Joe said.

They all followed him over to a computer, with the same analyst as the last time they'd been there.

"What'd you find out?" Bridge asked.

"First off, it's a connection we never would have

found out about if it hadn't been for you finding her the other day since she wasn't on our radar."

"Werther," Nicole said. "Or Dalton. Whatever she goes by."

"From here on out, I'm referring to her as Dalton since that's her real name."

"What'd she do?" Bridge asked.

"It's not as much what she did as much as who she met," Joe replied.

"Which was?"

"Abbott. Gary."

"They had a meeting?"

"Well, we cannot confirm they had a meeting as of this moment, but we can confirm they were in the same location at the same time. That definitely makes it suspicious."

"Where were they?"

"Greece. About two years ago."

"How do you know Dalton was there?"

"We confirmed it with MI6 just a little while ago. Since this now involves people from both agencies, we both came to the understanding that we would share whatever information we have on this matter. They gave us Dalton's itinerary for the last three years so we back-checked it against Abbott's movements."

"And how long ago was that?" Bridge asked.

"Two years. So over a year before Abbott was killed. Big coincidence, huh?"

"You know I don't believe in that."

"Me neither," Joe said. "But here's another. In tracing Dalton's history, we also discovered another crossover."

"What was that?"

"She was also in Ukraine. For about a month. Two years ago. It was exactly one month after she left Greece."

"Where Kenny was."

Joe nodded. "And also Magareth."

"So whatever they're doing, they've been doing it a while."

"And under the radar."

"Wait, let me understand the timeline on this," Nicole said. "So Abbott and Dalton meet in Greece about two years ago."

"Right."

"And then when she left there, she went to Ukraine, where Kenny and Magareth also were at that time?"

"Correct."

"That's it, then."

"What's that?" Joe asked.

"Whatever this is about has to do with Abbott in either the month before or the month after that meeting in Greece. Or whatever happened in Greece."

"What makes you so sure?"

"It stands to reason that whatever happened, he made some kind of deal with Dalton. She was the first one involved with him. Then she went to Ukraine to recruit the others."

"Possibly, but we cannot say for certain what that meeting was about. Could be anything at this point."

"Where was Abbott before and after that meeting?"

"Right before that, he was in Italy," Joe answered. "After leaving Greece, he went to Poland."

"Wait a minute," the analyst said, interrupting the conversation. "They met up again a few months after that."

"What?"

"They were in Greece again at the same time."

"When?"

"Two weeks before Abbott came home."

Joe looked at the others. "That's not a coincidence."

"No, it's not," Bridge said. "Greece is the target."

"Well, we still don't know that for sure."

Bridge sighed, then backed away from the others and started pacing the room. There were more things going through his mind.

"What is it?" Nicole asked.

Bridge stopped and folded his arms. His head shook a little as he tried to formulate his thoughts. "I still can't help but think we got this all wrong."

"How so?" Joe asked.

"All this time, we assumed this was about Abbott and a mole. Maybe it's Kenny, maybe someone else, and I just can't help but think this has nothing to do with that. Speaking of which, do you have any evidence that suggests anything he told you regarding a mole is true?"

"Just a lot of hearsay and rumors. He came through with some documents for us that never led anywhere."

"There's something else," Nicole said.

Bridge took a deep breath before continuing. "This is what I think, obviously without proof. I have a feeling that Abbott and Dalton came to some kind of agreement, probably with something illegal, and their plan was to throw off their activities by coming up with this bogus story of a mole. They'd know you were more worried about that than finding out about whatever they were doing."

"What about Kenny?"

"Well, I think that Dalton recruited him, and Magareth, when she went to Ukraine. All this time, we were going under the assumption that Kenny was the leader of this thing, probably because we were working under the theory that he was the mole. But if there is no mole, then that kind of takes him out of the picture. If he and Abbott never appeared together, then he's not the main guy."

"Unless he used a disguise and a different name to do that," Joe said.

"Always possible with a man like him. But I'm thinking this was something between Dalton and Abbott. She recruited the others."

"For what purpose?" Nicole asked.

Bridge shrugged. "Either she planned to betray

Abbott all along, or maybe she got them for protection, or maybe they just needed some extra help to pull off whatever they were doing. I'm not sure."

"That's a lot of good theories," Joe said. "But they're just that. Theories."

"But they make sense."

"They do. But we can't prove them anymore than we can prove the other ones we were working under."

Bridge then looked at Nicole. "I think it's time we booked a flight."

"Where we going?"

"Europe."

"Now hold on," Joe said. "If you're thinking of going over there to try to follow them, we don't know exactly where they are right now."

"I think we have a good idea."

"They flew into Paris. How's that play into it, if at all?"

"I don't think it does," Bridge asked. "If they think we're watching, they're not going to lead us directly to where they're going. They're going somewhere completely irrelevant."

"We still need to figure out who that fourth man is," Nicole said.

"Any ideas?"

"Not as yet," Joe replied. "Until we get some type of lead, could be anybody at this point. Could be someone that any one of them know that's not tied to the others."

"I still think we should go."

"As you may know, we do have teams over there."

"But none of them are me."

"Well, I can't argue with you there."

"And it's my client who's missing. No one else is going to have a bigger incentive to find him than I do."

"He's an American citizen, Luke. Last I checked, protecting them is part of our job description."

"But there's more in play than just that."

"You don't work for me. I can't tell you what you can or can't do."

"But you could give me support," Bridge said.

Joe smiled. "Are you offering your services in conjunction with an off-the-books CIA operation?"

Bridge nodded. "I guess I am."

"Well then... I guess I accept."

"What can you give me?"

"We have a substation in Athens. Go there. I'll alert them that you're coming. You'll get everything you need and complete cooperation."

"Assuming that's where these guys are going," Nicole said. "It's well over a full day from Paris to Greece by car."

"Maybe they drove into Italy or Germany, then took another flight under different names again," Bridge said.

"I guess anything's possible."

"You're convinced that Greece is the target here?" Joe asked.

"Not convinced. Just making an educated guess."

"Well then, we'll just have to keep digging here to make sure that that guess is supported then, won't we?"

"Yes, sir."

"How soon can you be ready?"

"We can be in the air by the end of today."

"Looks as though you two need to get moving then."

"I assume we'll need some identification?"

"When you get to the substation, you'll need a code phrase."

"What is it?"

"I'm an American tourist."

"His reply?"

"Aren't we all?"

Bridge looked at Nicole. "Looks like we're going on a trip."

16

Once Bridge and Nicole arrived in Greece, they immediately checked in at the CIA substation in Athens. They didn't even bother with a hotel first. They wanted to make sure they got off running as soon as they got on the ground. After going to the address that they were given, they stood outside of it. It was a small two-story building at the end of a shopping district.

"They sure picked their cover well with this place," Nicole said.

"That's the idea." Bridge looked around as scores of people walked past them. "Blend in."

They knocked on the door, and a man in his late twenties soon answered. He looked the part of a CIA agent. Big, muscular, short haircut, though dressed in shorts and a T-shirt.

"Help you?"

"I'm an American tourist," Bridge answered.

"Aren't we all?" the man looked at the two of them. "Both of you?"

"We're a package deal."

"Hey, the more the merrier. Come on in."

They went inside and followed the man upstairs to the second floor. They had a nice window view on the backside of the floor. Bridge and Nicole went over to it.

"Lovely view," Nicole said.

"Isn't it? Love working here." The man stuck his hand out to greet both of them. "I'm Steve."

"Luke. This is Nicole."

"Glad to meet both of you." Steve then introduced the other five members of the team who were all working at their desks.

"This all of you?"

"Yeah, we're a pretty small operation here, but we do a pretty good job of gathering intel."

"I'm assuming you were told we were coming," Bridge said.

"Absolutely. Pinnacle One told me himself. I've already been informed about the mission."

"How long you been stationed here?" Nicole asked.

"Two years. Best two years of my life."

"Lots of action?"

"Eh, some. The weather's the best, though. Can get a little hot at times during the summer, but I don't mind. Better than those crazy North Dakota winters where I'm from, that's for sure."

"You able to tell us anything about what we're here for?" Bridge asked.

"Well, I've been doing some digging. I wasn't brought into it before now. Was working on some other things."

"Find anything new?"

"Not as yet, but we're working on it."

"Any ideas on what they would be doing here?"

"Well, there's a few big issues here," Steve replied. "Greece is a gateway to Europe for traffickers smuggling drugs, cocaine, heroin, and some other stuff from the Middle East and southwest Asia. Then you also have chemicals going to the east. Then you also have some money laundering from organized crime and drug trafficking."

"What's the terrorist situation here?"

"Not much. There's the Revolutionary Struggle, a local group known for some government attacks, as well as at the American Embassy. The RS has been largely inactive the last couple years, though. A few shootouts with local police and all, but they haven't been much of a factor outside of that."

"You don't think they would be involved in this?" Nicole asked.

"I would doubt it. They're mostly a local group. They only operate inside Greece, and mostly in Athens. I can't see them being involved in all this other stuff that I'm hearing."

"What's your best guess?" Bridge asked.

"They don't pay me for guesses."

"They don't pay you to sit on your hands either."

Steve laughed. "True." He sat in his computer chair, put his elbow on the arm of the chair, and his hand over his mouth as he thought about it. "Based on what I know so far, if I had to guess, I'd say it has to do with some type of money laundering. Or just money in general."

"Why?"

"Well, does anything that you've come across so far indicate there's drugs involved?"

Bridge shook his head. "None."

"Then there you go. If they're coming to Greece, and there's no drugs, then it has to be about money. How long you guys figuring on staying?"

"Till it's done."

"Could be a long stay."

"I don't think so. People like this usually have a short timeline. They don't drag things out."

Steve nodded. "Maybe so. I noticed you had some bags with you. Find a place to stay yet?"

"No, we came here first. Wanted to see if you had anything for us yet."

"Oh. Sorry to disappoint. Why don't you guys get settled, then come back over?"

"Where's a good place to go?"

"Well, we're all within twenty minutes walking distance of here, spread out. You know how it is about everyone staying in the same location."

"Yeah."

"Anyway, there's a spot up the street if you like. Maybe ten minutes away. I'll take you over."

"Sounds good."

Kenny was the first to arrive at the house. He went inside and checked it out to make sure there were no surprise visitors waiting for them. With it being clear, he went out front to wait for the others. Another car pulled up about twenty minutes later. Dalton, Magareth, Abbott, and the man that picked them up at the airport arrived. His name was Argus Kanelos, a native of Greece. He was the first to be brought in on the scheme that Dalton and Gary Abbott had developed.

Once they were all out of the car, Magareth shoved a rifle into Abbott's back to get him moving.

"Took you long enough," Kenny said.

"You've been here maybe twenty minutes, tops," Dalton said. "I don't wanna hear how long you've been waiting."

She led the others inside. "Nice place," Magareth said, looking around. "I'm digging it."

"It's been in the family for three generations," Kanelos said. "So please, don't make a mess."

They went out back where there was a large rectangular-shaped in-ground swimming pool.

"Let's get this over with," Kenny said.

"I've told you repeatedly," Dalton said. "We have two days before we're able to retrieve the money. We can't take it out before then."

"I don't see what difference it makes."

"Because there are codes and rules that must be abided by. They will be honored."

"Honor among thieves?"

"Something like that."

"How much money are we talking, anyway?"

"It doesn't matter," Dalton answered. "You've been promised your cut, and you shall get it. All you need to do is provide security. Everything else is on me."

Everyone started going down their separate paths. Magareth stayed close to Abbott to make sure he didn't try to escape. Dalton was somewhat sympathetic to Abbott's situation, even though she was the one who was responsible for it, and waved Magareth off his post.

"You can ease up," Dalton said. "He's not going anywhere. Go have a sandwich or something."

Magareth was chewing on some gum. He looked down at Abbott for a second. The man hadn't provided any problems thus far, so he didn't think leaving him alone for a little while would be an issue. Magareth nodded and went inside, leaving just Dalton and Abbott alone. Abbott's hands were tied together in front of him, but Dalton removed his restraints. She sat next to him as they faced the pool.

"I'm sorry for all the treatment," Dalton said. "But as long as you do what is asked of you, I give you my word that you will be released unharmed when it's all over."

Abbott was silent for a moment, unsure if he should say anything. But he wanted to know. "It's been like a week since you guys took me. You still haven't told me what you want with me."

Dalton took a deep breath, wondering if she should reveal her plans yet. She decided it was time to let him know what she needed him for, since he had a part to play.

"I knew your brother."

"Did you kill him?" Abbott asked.

Dalton hesitated before answering. "No. But Kenny did."

"Why? What did he do to you?"

Dalton snickered. "Why is a very complicated issue. I didn't want him dead."

"So why'd you do it?"

"It was done without my consent. I never would've let that happen if I had known about his intentions."

"That still doesn't explain why. Why was he killed? What did he ever do to you?"

"How well did you know your brother?"

"Pretty well. He travelled a lot, so we didn't see each other that much, but we talked on the phone, texted, emailed pretty regularly."

"And did he ever mention me?"

"No."

"There's quite a bit that you don't know about him."

"Like what?"

"He was... being used by the CIA to help funnel information to them. He was also using his business as a salesman as a front."

"How would you know any of that?"

"Because we were... involved," Dalton said.

"What?"

"Your brother and I had a relationship that lasted over six months."

"You and him? He never said anything."

"I didn't suppose he would."

"But if you were... then why did..."

"I was once employed by MI6. I had an assignment here in Greece. That's where I met Gary. I won't bore you with the details about my mission, but it's safe to say that I was very disillusioned with my job satisfaction at that point. I devised a plan to get away from it all. I needed money to make that happen. And I knew where I could get it."

"Where does Gary fit in?"

"He wanted to help me. I told him how frustrated I'd become, what I wanted, and he offered to help me. And I let him. Because I loved him."

"I still don't understand."

"There was an illegal drug trafficking ring being run out of Ukraine. That's where I met those other guys. Anyway, without getting into a lot of those boring details, we basically took a bunch of money and merchandise from this group."

"You mean you stole it?"

Dalton shrugged. "I guess you can call it whatever you like. We took what we wanted."

"And Gary helped with all this?"

"He did. He did it for me. For us. Once I disappeared, he was going to come with me."

"He never said a word."

"He couldn't. He was already involved with the CIA at that point. Anyway, we sold the drugs for cash, but we had to move quickly. The group we took everything from was onto us and closing in. We had to split up, stash the money, then go our separate ways for a while."

"What does that mean?"

"We stashed the money in a local bank here," Dalton replied. "Well, it's not a real bank. It's basically run by criminals for criminals. It's almost like a safe house. It's heavily guarded by armed men and you can't get inside without a pass, which you receive when you drop money off."

"What's that got to do with me?"

"You may find this hard to believe with a place like that, but there are certain rules you must abide by to use their services. One, they take a cut of whatever money is deposited once it's taken out. Two, whoever deposits the money must also be there to take it out. It's a way to be sure there's no double-crossing beforehand. Though I guess that doesn't preclude anyone from killing the other when it's removed. Anyway, Gary and I were both there. I needed him to withdraw the money."

"So why have him killed?"

"I didn't want him killed. I wanted him. I needed him. He'd been having second thoughts about everything. He didn't want to come back over. He thought we could start a new life without it. I tried to explain that for someone like me to disappear, for us to disappear, we needed a lot of money to make that happen. There's new identities, new passports, cars, houses, plus money to pick up and move if we were ever compromised. You can't do that on a shoestring budget. You need millions to make sure you're comfortable."

"I don't understand what's going on. If you needed Gary to take the money out, what am I doing here?"

"You're going to take his place."

"What?"

"You look similar. They'll require your signature, which you'll have to match up with Gary's."

"We don't sound alike."

"It's fine. Gary only said one word when we were there. They won't remember."

"I don't know..."

"Chris, you have to do this. I loved Gary. He'd want you to do this for me."

A look of confusion appeared in Abbott's eyes. "But, I don't…"

"Just help me get the money out, and I'll make sure you get back home safely and with something extra in your pocket too."

"Why did Kenny kill him?"

"As I said, Gary was having second thoughts about it. Kenny followed him back to New York. They apparently had some words, Gary said he was through, and Kenny killed him. It was all done without my knowledge. I wouldn't have let that happen to Gary if I had known. You have to believe that."

"But why wait so long? Gary died over a year ago."

"One of the rules of the bank is that you have to wait six months before withdrawing the money. I believe they also use the money for other things in the meantime, though for what I'm not exactly sure. It's probably not legal. Anyway, I thought after Gary's death it would be prudent to wait another six months or so to let the heat die down a little. I figured if enough time had passed, everyone would forget about this. And it probably would have too if you hadn't kept trying to keep your brother's name alive."

"I just wanted to know what happened."

"I know. And I wish I could've told you. Maybe I should have, I don't know. Can't really do anything about that now."

Abbott sat there, somewhat stunned, staring at the clear blue water of the pool. He could hardly believe

any of this. In his wildest dreams—or nightmares—
none of this is what he could have expected to find
when he started poking around into his brother's
death.

"So his death didn't have anything to do with the
CIA? They were saying something about him finding a
mole in the agency."

"No," Dalton said. "That was just a cover story that
we made up."

"You made it up?"

"Gary knew that the agency was using him. They
didn't care about him. They were using him for information and when they were done with him, or he
outlived his usefulness to them, they'd just throw him
away. In order for us to help cover our tracks and
prevent anyone, the CIA, MI6, anyone, we came up
with a plan. We decided to invent a story about a mole
within the CIA's ranks. We planted a similar story
within MI6. We even created documents to help
support that."

"It was all fake?"

"Yes. It was all done to prevent anyone from
looking into our activities within Ukraine and here.
They'd be more worried about finding a possible mole
within their ranks."

"It's unbelievable."

"Seems to have worked too, because a year later,
from what I understand, they're still looking at mole
targets."

"I just can't believe it."

Dalton put her hand on Abbott's knee. "Chris, all you have to do is accompany me to this bank. You'll put down your signature, we take out the money, we split it with the others, and you can go back home. Then you can at least have the knowledge of what really happened with your brother."

"But what about them? If they know I know they killed Gary then..."

"Don't worry about them. I can take care of them. And if it ever comes down to them versus you, well, you're Gary's brother. I owe it to him to protect you. Don't worry. You can trust me."

17

B ridge was still at the hotel, on the phone with a few contacts, hoping he could get some kind of lead on their targets. Nicole was already at the substation, working on a computer as she waited for him. As she typed away, Steve took a seat next to her and also started working. Work wasn't really what he had on his mind, though. It wasn't every day there was someone as pretty as Nicole sitting next to him.

"So... uh... what's up with you and Luke?"

Nicole stopped typing, thinking the question was strange. She turned her head toward him. "What?"

"You and Luke. Are you guys... you know, together or anything?"

"Now why would you ask that?"

"Well, you came in together, at the same hotel and all. I was just wondering if you and him were..."

"He's taken. Sorry."

"Oh, no, I didn't mean... I mean, that's all good and all. I don't have any problem with people who go that way, but..."

Nicole smiled. "I know what you meant."

"Oh. So, uh, if he's taken, then maybe you and I could go somewhere later? Maybe somewhere quiet without a lot of lighting?"

"Why without lighting? Embarrassed about something?"

"Oh, no, no, not at all. Nothing to be ashamed about here. I just thought that... you know, you're very attractive, and you're probably not going to be here very long, so, maybe we could take advantage of the moment."

"Listen, Steve, you seem like a nice guy, and I'm sure a lot of women around these parts find you attractive, but when I said Luke's taken, I meant he's taken by me. And that means vice versa, too."

Steve put his hands up. "Hey, no worries, not trying to cut in on anyone's turf or anything. Just figured I'd take a shot."

Nicole smiled. "Find anything interesting yet today?"

"No, I just got here a little while ago myself, but we're pretty much still in a holding pattern. Something will break. It always does."

"Question is, will it break in time for us to do something about it? And before Chris Abbott ends up on the side of the road somewhere?"

Bridge came into the building a few seconds later, looking like he was out of breath.

"You all right?" Nicole asked.

"Got here as quick as I could."

"Why? Someone chasing you?"

"No. Was just on the phone with Pinnacle One. Said to get over here right away. Said they got a lead for us and wanted to wait until we were all here to share it."

Steve immediately dialed their New York number to get a video conference going. There was a huge sixty-five-inch monitor on one of the walls that they all turned to. A minute later, Joe appeared on the screen.

"Everyone ready?" Joe asked.

"We're all here, Chief," Steve replied.

"Good. A few hours ago, we finally got a hit on our mysterious fourth man." A picture of Kanelos appeared on the screen. "His name is Argus Kanelos. He's a Greek national. He comes from a wealthy family, though he himself has done very little to expand on that fortune. All he's really done with it is spend it."

"How do we know that's him?" Bridge asked.

"We got him on a surveillance camera in Italy. He was behind the wheel of the same car we saw at the Paris airport."

"So they did drive all the way here," Nicole said.

"Most likely they didn't want to take the risk of getting spotted at another airport and giving their exact location away. It's a thirty-hour drive from Paris to Athens with no stops. If they took turns at the wheel, might have been more preferable to them than taking a plane to get there faster."

"What about this Kanelos?" Bridge asked.

"His family owns a string of houses all over Greece. It's possible the gang's using one of them, assuming they're actually in the country and we haven't got it all wrong. Now, we've already compiled a list of addresses that his family owns, so I would say our next move is for you guys to hit those houses and see if they're there."

"How do you want us to work it, Chief?" Steve asked.

"Well, time is of the essence on this, so with that in mind, I would say to split up into two teams of four. You'll cover more ground that way. And you're looking at four targets. I don't want any smaller number of teams going up against them if we can help it. They're a very dangerous group. Luke and Nicole can attest to that. You'll have to be on your toes. Any objections with that?"

"None here, Chief."

"Good."

"Should we inform the locals and have them go along with us?"

"No. I want this handled in-house. They don't know you're there right now, and I'd prefer to keep it that way. You've provided some good intel while stationed there, I don't wanna blow that cover over this. You guys take care of this. This is an all-hands-on-deck situation. Everyone's to drop what they're doing and handle this. This is our top priority at the moment."

"Understood."

"We'll send over all the photos that we got from the cameras so you can look at them. Keep me updated as you move along."

"Will do." Steve looked at the others. "So you two physically ran into them already?"

Bridge instinctively put his hand on the back of his head. "Yeah. Didn't turn out so well."

"They the shoot first and ask questions later type of people?"

"They definitely are."

Steve went over to one of the other men in the room. "Put those pictures on screen as soon as we get them."

"They're coming through now," the man replied.

Steve went back to his seat as the pictures came on the monitor.

"There's Kanelos driving," Bridge said, pointing to him.

"Tough to make out the other ones," Steve said.

"Well, that's Dalton in the front passenger seat."

"Can't really see who's in the back too well," Nicole said.

"It's clear enough. You can't see faces, but you can see bodies. And you can see three of them."

"That means one of them is Abbott."

Bridge nodded. "Assuming the other two in the back are Kenny and Magareth, yeah, he's still alive."

"What do they want with this guy?" Steve asked.

"I think that's gonna be your job to track that down."

"Huh?"

"They obviously need him for something specific, otherwise they would have dumped his body long ago. And they need him for something here in Greece. What is it?"

Steve leaned back in his chair and put his hand over his mouth as he thought. He could only shake his head. He couldn't think of anything specifically. Then the list of houses that the Kanelos family owned appeared on the screen. There were eight of them. And they were spread all over the country.

"Looks like we each take four," Steve said.

"How far away are all of these?"

"They're scattered, man. A couple of these are about eight or nine hours away. A couple are closer."

"I guess we should start with the closest and work from there."

"Yeah. I'll take you two with me. I'll get the other team started. I'll have them start with the ones further away while we take the closer ones."

As Steve was talking to his other men, Nicole sat down and plugged Kanelos' name into the computer. A fairly decent list of things popped up on his report. He was known to skirt on the opposite side of the law, though nothing as big as this before. He mostly stuck to the drug trade.

"How's this guy factor into this?" Nicole asked.

"Maybe he's trying to step up in class."

"Maybe."

"Or maybe he's not really involved much other than them using him for a place or transportation," Bridge said. "Since he hasn't been with the others, it could indicate he's not in as deep as them."

"Something else on your mind?"

"I dunno. Just seems like we're not gonna find these guys by knocking over houses. Seems like we need to figure out what they're planning; what they're up to. And we still don't have a clue yet."

"Who knows? Maybe we'll get lucky."

"Yeah. Maybe."

Steve came over to them a minute later. "Gun cabinet's over here." He led them over to the large army green cabinet. "Take your pick."

Bridge and Nicole both took a rifle as well as a handgun, along with some extra ammo. If they did find Dalton and the others, they were fairly sure they wouldn't come along quietly.

"If we find these guys, sounds like the most action we'll have had here in a while," Steve said energetically, a huge smile on his face like he was actually looking forward to running into their targets. "Let's do this. You guys ready?"

Bridge looked at Nicole, a little surprised at the

enthusiasm. He'd been through too many of these to get that excited over them anymore. He gave her a shrug.

"Yeah, sure. I'm ready."

"Me too," Nicole said.

Steve continued smiling with a slight nod. "Let's rock-and-roll."

18

They were down to their last house. They'd
started searching these houses almost twenty-
four hours before. So far, everything had come up
empty. A couple of the houses were empty, but there
were no signs anyone was actually living there. And a
few of the houses actually had people living there, but
there were no signs their targets were among them. For
the houses that had people in them, they sat on those
for a while, making sure they could rule them out.

Now, they were sitting in their car, their eyes on the
last remaining house. There were no cars parked in
front. Of course, that didn't mean no one was inside.
They could have ditched the car. Or one of them might
have been out using it with the others still in there. Or
they could have left entirely, leaving a clue behind. The
only thing they didn't hope for was that it was the

wrong house completely. They had been watching it for close to thirty minutes, not a sign of life anywhere. A few of them were starting to get impatient.

"I say we move," Steve said.

"I agree," Nicole replied. "We're not getting anywhere just sitting here."

They both looked at Bridge to see what he thought. For once, he really didn't have an opinion either way. He looked at the both of them and shrugged. He was OK with either choice.

"Let's take it down," Steve said. "Even if no one's there, then we can move on. We can't be wasting time here on an empty house."

Bridge nodded, then checked his weapon. "Ready."

"Everyone good?"

Once everyone said they were, they all got out of the car. The house was in the middle of a residential neighborhood. Not exactly the best location for someone who wanted to stay hidden. But like they always said, sometimes the best spot to hide was in the middle of a crowd. As they approached the house, they looked around to make sure they weren't spotted. Steve and his partner took the front, while Bridge and Nicole made their way around to the back. Still no sign of anything.

"You good back there?" Steve asked.

"Ready when you are," Bridge replied.

"Let's move."

Steve and his partner broke through the front door while Bridge and Nicole went through the back. With guns locked in front of their bodies, they swept through the house, going room by room. Within a few minutes, every room had been checked. There was nothing there. Not even an empty candy wrapper. They checked the refrigerator. If someone had been there, they took everything with them. They put their guns away and convened in the living room.

"The last house on the list," Steve said. "It doesn't make sense."

Bridge sighed. "It really does if you think about it."

"How's that?"

"If they're using Kanelos for his access to places to stay, if they know we're on to them, they might think we'll find out Kanelos is the last guy on the team."

"And they'd know we'd run a check on him and find all these houses."

"So they know we're gonna go around spinning our wheels checking these places out that they never had any intention on being in. It keeps us busy chasing ghosts while they go in a different direction, putting even more time between them and us."

"Smart."

"These guys ain't dumb."

"That also means we're no closer than when we started."

"Yeah."

"Let's get back to base and try to figure this out from a new angle."

Bridge nodded, though he wasn't sure what else there was to learn. They needed a break. A big one. And he wasn't sure it was coming. But they went back to the station anyway, hoping something would fall into their lap.

The crew was stirring. Dalton woke up and walked around the house, looking out the windows, making sure there was nothing suspicious going on. She didn't want any surprise guests showing up.

"There's no one there," Kenny said. "We've got this."

"It won't take long before the CIA realizes what we're doing."

"By the time they do, we'll be long gone. They're probably still checking Kanelos' houses right now." He laughed. "Idiots."

"And when they find nothing there, they'll move on to something else."

"Like I said, we'll be gone by then. We only need one more day."

Dalton's head quickly spun around. There was a frantic look in her eyes. She had seen Magareth, who was in the same room as Abbott, guarding him. But she hadn't seen the last member of the team.

"Where is he?"

"He went out for a bit," Kenny said.

"What?!"

Kenny shrugged. "Said he was bored and wanted to get something to eat."

"We have food here."

"I dunno. Said something about some restaurant that he knows that's close by. They have some local dish that he was craving or something."

"That idiot! I specifically said for everyone to stay here and not go anywhere until we had to."

"Said he'd only be gone an hour or two."

"And you let him go?"

"Relax. Everything will be fine."

"And what if someone recognizes him or the car he's driving, and he leads them back here?"

"You worry too much."

"And you're not worrying enough. Or thinking, apparently."

"Who cares about him? Who needs him, anyway? What's he good for at this point? He's served his purpose."

"Everyone was promised an equal share for their service."

Kenny leaned forward, putting his arms on the table in front of him. "But everyone's not pulling an equal weight. Why should he get the same share as the rest of us? All he's done is drive us around and give us a house to stay in. We don't even need him from this point."

Dalton folded her arms as she looked out the window. She couldn't deny that Kanelos was a loose end. As much as she was angry at him, though, she still didn't like the thought of eliminating him.

"C'mon," Kenny said. "That money will stretch a lot farther for both of us if we don't have to share some of it. We both know it."

"There's still plenty."

"We're talking a ten-million-dollar payday. Now, you're taking half of that, which I'm good with it. It's your deal, so you should get that. But five million split three ways isn't as appealing as splitting it in two."

"We may need him for some reason after we withdraw the money."

Kenny nodded. He could understand that reasoning. Just in case the CIA or anyone else somehow caught up with them, an extra gun to have in the fight would be nice. But in the event that they didn't need it, he wasn't hearing her say no.

"And what about the little guy?"

Dalton stopped looking out the window and turned toward him. "Chris?"

"What are we gonna do with him?"

Dalton shrugged. "Send him on his way."

"You're serious?"

"After this is over, he can't hurt us."

"The hell he can't. He'll know what we did, where we went, and he'll know about that bank."

"So? We'll never be using it again. And who cares if he knows what we did? He won't know where we're going."

"We both know what we need to do with him."

"No. That doesn't need to happen."

"Know what I think?"

"I don't really happen to care what you think."

"I think you got a soft spot for him," Kenny said. "I think because you had a thing for his brother, and his brother's now dead. Maybe you can't do what you know needs to be done."

"Because it doesn't need to be done."

"Loose ends. We both know in this business loose ends get you killed. And he's a loose end."

"I'll take care of him."

"How?"

"I don't know. I'll give him a little money or something."

"That ain't coming out of my share."

"I'll take care of it. Is that OK with you?"

Kenny stared at her for a few moments. He then shrugged. "We wouldn't even be having this problem if you could've kept yourself in check."

"Oh, you talking about Gary now? Is that what you're doing? You didn't have to kill him."

"He wanted out. He wasn't coming back here. He wasn't helping us anymore. And most of all, he didn't want you anymore. And you still haven't accepted that."

"I could've talked to him. I could've convinced him."

"Bullshit. He was done. He was having second thoughts, and he didn't want anything to do with anyone anymore. Not you, not me, and not the money. He was out."

"I still could've talked him into it."

"You're deluding yourself. What you had with him was gone. You had a nice few months with him and thought you were living the fairy tale. But guess what? You put your slippers on at midnight and the dream was over. And you haven't come to grips with that yet."

"Go to hell."

"I've already been there. Remember what I said about loose ends? Gary had become a loose end. He wasn't willing to help us anymore. All he could do was hurt us."

"He wouldn't have talked."

"And you know that how? He was working for the CIA, for Christ's sake. You think he wouldn't at some point reveal how that whole mole storyline shit was a bunch of crap? You think he really wouldn't say what this whole thing was really about at some point? He was a loose end. You know it. And in this business, loose ends need to be dealt with. I knew you weren't going to do it, so I did what had to be done. I dealt with it."

Dalton turned her attention back out the window. She didn't really want to hear anymore. It was all hitting too close to home. Everything Kenny was saying was probably correct, but that didn't make it easy to hear. She didn't want to. She still wanted to believe she and Gary had something special and would've continued to have it.

"You need to cut the crap, Zara." Kenny stood up, ready to leave the room. "You're a former MI6 agent, for crying out loud. You're the best of the best. It's time you start acting like it. Loose ends get you killed in this business. But you know what else does? Soft spots. Abbott needs to be cut loose. If you won't do it, then I will."

Kenny then walked out of the room. Dalton looked at him as he disappeared. She was angry. She looked out the window again, hoping to gain some clarity in her own mind. Everything was going through it: Gary, Chris, Kanelos, Kenny, the money. What Kenny had told her wasn't pleasant to hear, but maybe she should have listened to it. Maybe he wasn't wrong.

Dalton then went into the other room, where Magareth was watching Abbott. She stood there for a moment, watching her lover's brother, thinking about the future. Kenny's words still raced through her mind. She wasn't sure she could do it, though. She didn't want to do it.

"You can go," Dalton said. Magareth looked up at her. "I'll watch him for a bit. Get some rest."

Magareth nodded. He wasn't about to argue with her. He was tired of watching Abbott, anyway. Not that Abbott had given any problems, because he had complied with their wishes every step of the way, but it would be nice to stretch his legs without having to worry about where their prisoner was. As Magareth left the room, Dalton took the same seat against the wall, with Abbott sitting against the adjoining wall.

"You hungry?" Dalton asked.

"No."

"This will all be over soon."

"I just want to go home."

"I know. By this time tomorrow, we'll have everything we need. And then it will be over."

"And what about me?"

"What about you?"

"What are you going to do with me?" Abbott asked.

"I told you before. After it's done, you can go."

"What about Kenny? He killed my brother. I get the feeling he wants to do the same to me."

"Don't worry about that. Just worry about playing your part and helping me get the money. After that, everything will take care of itself."

"And Kenny?"

"I have control of him. He'll do what I tell him."

Abbott felt only slightly better. Though he honestly believed that Dalton meant everything she said, he didn't get the same feeling about Kenny. He seemed like the type of guy who did what he wanted, regardless of what he was told, or what anyone else wanted.

"Are you sure about that?"

"Positive," Dalton said. "He'll do what he's told. He'll do what has to be done." Dalton thought about it a few more seconds. "And so will I."

19

Bridge, Nicole, and the rest of the team were at the substation, trying to dig up any leads that they could. Though they couldn't be sure of any timelines, it felt like they were running out of time. A call then came in from New York. Joe's face came on the monitor. Everyone scrambled away from their desks and stood in front of it as he started speaking.

"While you guys were house hunting, we've been doing some background work on Argus Kanelos," Joe said.

"Find anything interesting?" Bridge asked.

"Plenty. And we may have figured out what's going on here. Or at least part of it."

"What do you got?"

"We've uncovered several communications between Kanelos and another email address that we have still yet to figure out who is behind it."

"What did they say?"

"Well, first of all, we're assuming the email account he's conversing with belongs to either Dalton or Kenny."

"Why?"

"The emails were opened through an IP address that registers to a location in Ukraine."

"At the time they were both there, I take it?"

"You guessed it."

"Is it possible they were using a VPN to disguise their real location and maybe just incriminating one of those people?" Nicole asked.

"No, that's a good call, though. Best as we can determine, the location is as legit as it gets."

"But we can't pinpoint who it was exactly?" Bridge asked.

"Negative. At least not as yet. We're still working on it, though. We'll get there."

"How long ago were these emails?"

"The first ones we've got are from last year. We've got a few spread out since then, the latest of which we have is from last month."

"You said you thought you knew what this was about?"

"In the exchange of emails, they go into several different topics, one is nailing down some type of housing situation for whoever Kanelos is talking to."

"Housing?"

"Yes. We'll send a few of the emails over to you so

you can examine them, but the gist of it is they wanted Kanelos to find suitable housing for them for a period of one to three days."

"We've checked every house the Kanelos family owns. There's no sign of any of them being there. If they were in one of the empty ones, they left no clues behind that they were there, and if they were in one of the ones being rented, there was nothing to suggest they were being hidden."

"That's because they didn't use any of those," Joe said. "In the emails, Kanelos was explicitly told not to use any house that can be traced back to the family."

Steve stepped up to ask a question. "Then what sense does it make to use Kanelos at all if they're not using his family connections? I mean, he's definitely no angel, but he's definitely not up to the caliber of the rest of the people he's hobnobbing with either. It doesn't make sense."

"It makes a little more sense if you come to the realization that they're probably just using Kanelos to find an adequate house, help with whatever they need with Abbott, and in getting the money."

"Money?" Bridge asked. "What money?"

"In several of the emails they reference a place called The Brick."

"The Brick?" Bridge looked at the others to see if they knew the reference. Nicole shook her head, but by the look on Steve's face, he understood it. "What's The Brick?"

"Steve can probably fill you in a little better after we're finished here, but for now, you need to know that The Brick is a large building, basically referenced to as a bank, designed for criminals, run by criminals, and used by criminals of all nationalities. Every government intelligence agency knows it exists."

Bridge put his hands up. "If everyone knows about it, how's it allowed to operate?"

"There may be a few people in either the police or government agencies that have a hand in the cookie jar, so to speak. We don't need to debate the hows and whys right now. At this moment, the only thing we need to concern ourselves with, is whether that's the target that Dalton and Kenny have. And since they've mentioned the name, which is basically forbidden unless you have business with it, we believe that it is."

"What about a date and a time? How's this system work?"

"A date and time we don't know. But considering they're there, which is where The Brick is located, we've got to believe that it's happening soon."

"Is that why they need Abbott?"

"We still don't know. The inner workings of it are still somewhat of a mystery, but it's a good guess that they need him for something."

"It's gotta have something to do with it," Nicole said. "There's no other reason for it."

"Where's this place at?" Bridge asked.

"Steve will fill you in on the details," Joe said. "But

it's in a remote area, and it's surrounded by guards. And plenty of them."

Bridge smiled, already knowing the answer to his next question. "By guards, I assume you mean heavily armed mercenaries who shoot anyone who's not authorized to come near the place?"

"That about covers it."

"I take it that means we're gonna have to stake this place out to see if our friends show up?"

"That's about the size of it."

"What about the alternate housing they directed Kanelos to find?" Nicole asked. "How 'bout zeroing in on that and see if we can find out where they are?"

"We've been trying, but we haven't been able to lock anything down yet. The theory we're going with is that we believe they used Kanelos to find an appropriate spot, probably away from the hustle and bustle of a big city, a place they could settle into without any prying eyes while they wait for whatever it is they're waiting for. They probably also directed him to do it under the radar."

"So nothing that we're going to be able to attach with his name on it," Bridge said.

"Most likely not. We're still checking, but like I said, it's unlikely we're going to be able to lock anything down definitively."

"Seems like a lot of loose pieces on this," Steve said. "Sounds like they've got two extra parts they don't need."

"No, don't discount anything. They need them for a reason. Maybe to get into the bank, maybe to get out, maybe to help keep us off our toes. But they need them."

"They might be using Kanelos now to dump him later," Nicole said. "No loose ends."

"Quite possible. But for now, with the absence of their current address, we're gonna need eyes on that bank."

"Just out of curiosity, what's the advantage of using this bank to begin with?" Bridge asked.

"Convenience. It's mostly used by people who are either in a hurry, or want to hide their money. If you're on the run and can't take a large stash with you for whatever reason, you can deposit it there and come back for it later."

"Any chance the money won't be there?"

"None. It's there. The bank has a stellar reputation —if you can believe that—in the underworld community. They do what they say they'll do. They'll hold your money for a fee."

"What about this bank, Chief?" Steve asked. "You want us to hit it?"

"No. That bank has dozens of guards, both on the perimeter and inside the building. They're prepared in case of an attack. I do not want any type of firefight in that area. We are not there to wage war on that bank."

"Has it ever been hit before?" Bridge asked. "Just out of curiosity."

"It has. Several times. You can imagine if the place is known, some people will think they can get an easy score and help themselves. And from the fact that it's still there, you can guess what happened to the people who tried to hit it."

"So if we see Dalton and the others go into or out of the bank?" Steve asked.

"Let it happen. Follow them. See where they're going next. Whatever you do, make sure that you do not engage at that bank. If you do, you'll not only have Kenny and Dalton firing at you, you'll have the wrath of twenty other guards as well. And there's no backup coming to help you. At least not in time to save you if something goes wrong."

"Understood, Chief."

"And with that, I'll leave you ladies and gentlemen so you can have some time to devise a plan and strategy."

"Thank you, sir."

After Joe disappeared from the screen, Bridge immediately turned to Steve with some burning questions.

"Did you know about this bank?" Bridge asked.

"Yeah, but I had no reason to believe that's what they were doing here."

"What do you know about this place?"

"Pretty much what Joe said. It's a very secretive place."

"But you know where it is?"

"Yeah."

"How much time we got?"

"It's gonna be a drive," Steve answered.

"So we're already behind the eight ball."

"For all we know, they're hitting it as we speak."

Nicole cut into the conversation. "So if this is what their plan is, what do they need Chris for?"

"My guess?" Bridge said. "They need him to take the place of his brother."

"Why?"

Bridge shrugged. "Although this bank isn't on the up and up, it sounds as if it still has some stringent rules in regard to using it."

"That's true from what we hear," Steve said.

"So my guess is that either Gary deposited by himself, or with Dalton or Kenny, I'm not sure, but they need Chris' face. Or a signature. Or something like that. Or maybe they cloned Gary's fingerprint. But my guess is that they need Chris to get that money out."

"If that's the case, then at one point, Gary was with them," Nicole said.

Bridge nodded. "I would say that's likely. Now, whether he turned on them or decided he didn't want to go through with it anymore, or they just decided to cut him out, or whatever the reason, they decided to cut bait and kill him. Now, they're ready to take the money out, and they need Chris to do it."

"Which also means that when they do, they won't need Chris anymore."

Bridge sighed. "Yeah."

"Which means we gotta find them before they get out of that bank."

"It's unlikely they'll do it right then and there. Whoever runs that bank isn't going to look too fondly at a body being dumped on their doorstep, especially one that was just used to take money from them. They'll most likely wait a while."

"It ain't gonna be too long, though," Steve said.

"No, it won't."

"Sentiment's still the same. We need to have eyes on them coming out of that bank. 'Cause while they won't kill him right outside of the bank, they're not gonna wait hours either."

"We need to gear up now," Bridge said. "While we still have a chance."

20

The bank, or The Brick as it was commonly called, was nestled in a remote area not too far from the border of Bulgaria. There was only one dirt road leading to it. It was a quiet area. From where the team was in Athens, it was roughly a nine-hour drive to get to it. Since trying to remain hidden was a big factor, only Bridge, Nicole, and Steve went on the trip. The rest of the team was either still in Athens, trying to monitor everything from there, and a couple were on standby notice not too far away. If something got hairy and Bridge and company needed a rescue, they would be there to lend a hand.

Without knowing exactly where guards were placed along this road, and their proximity to the bank, the team only travelled about halfway up it before deciding to get out and move amongst the trees, using them as cover. It took another half hour on foot before the building was within their sights. They got down on their stomachs, making sure they were almost completely concealed within the brush and foliage. They got out their binoculars to survey the building and the surroundings.

"That's a bank?" Bridge asked, surprised about the appearance. "Looks more like the hunting quarters of some mountain men."

"I think it's supposed to look that way," Nicole said. "That way if anyone stumbles upon it, they won't know what's inside."

Bridge then looked at the armed guards stationed all around. "Yeah, 'cause the men with guns won't give anything away."

"How many you make out?" Steve asked. "I count eight so far."

Bridge scanned the compound with his binoculars. "I got twelve."

"Well, it's a good thing we're not trying to breach it."

"There's a bunch of cars out there," Nicole said.

"Yeah, but no telling whose they are. Could be visitors, could be the men that work there."

Bridge continued looking at the building, trying to find a window to look through. "We just need to hope that one of those cars belongs to Kenny or Dalton."

There were a few windows in the building, but they were darkly tinted, and seeing inside was difficult.

Bridge thought he detected some movement in a couple of them, but seeing who it was was nearly impossible from his vantage point. About ten minutes went by without any movement, except the guards who wandered around from time to time.

"Wait a minute," Nicole said. "We got movement by the front door."

They all put their binoculars on the front door, which was now halfway open, though nobody was visible. It had to be opened from the inside.

"Here we go. People coming out."

They all anxiously looked at the three people exiting the building. Their hopes were quickly dashed, as none of the three were anyone they recognized.

"Well, didn't figure it'd be that easy anyway," Steve said. "Would've been something if we got it on the first shot."

"I'm just hoping they weren't here and gone already," Bridge said.

"If they were, it's gonna be hell finding them. By the time we give up here, they'll have a long head start on us."

"They'll be here," Nicole said.

"What makes you so sure?" Steve asked.

"I can just feel it."

"Oh no, not that intuition thing again," Bridge said.

Nicole smiled. "Why not? It's always worked for me before."

"It has not. You just got lucky those other times."

"Jealous again."

"I'm not jealous."

"You just hate it when I'm right and you're wrong."

"I don't hate it. And for the record, I didn't say you were wrong about anything, not even here."

"Well, you're thinking it."

"I'm not thinking it."

"You guys married?" Steve asked.

"No!" Bridge and Nicole both replied in unison.

Steve looked at the two of them, not sure if they were telling the truth about that one. They sure sounded married. Or at least like a couple that had been together for fifty years.

"Oh," Steve said. "OK."

Nicole looked at her boyfriend and shook her head.

"What was that for?" Bridge asked.

"You know."

"No, I don't know."

"Can we just focus on the bank," Steve said.

"I am focusing," Nicole replied.

"You guys do this often?"

"Do what?" Bridge asked.

"Um, you know, like, argue?"

"We're not arguing."

"Not even close," Nicole said.

"Oh," Steve said. "Sounds like arguing."

"We're just expressing our feelings to each other."

Steve looked confused. "Oh."

"Having these kinds of discussions with each other helps to keep us loose and on our toes," Bridge said.

"It does?"

"Yeah. If you're really serious all the time, with the things you do, you'll just blow yourself up after a while."

"That wouldn't be good."

"No. So we like to keep things light."

"Makes sense. Pinnacle One highly regards you. When he informed me you were coming, he said you were one of the best he's ever seen."

"Always good to know," Bridge said.

"How come you're not still with the agency then?"

"Just got tired. Tired of risking my life and getting shot at, stabbed, poisoned, and blown up."

"But you're still here doing the same thing."

Bridge laughed, appreciating the irony. "Yeah. Funny, isn't it?"

"Yeah."

"Only thing now is I get to decide what I'm gonna get shot at over instead of someone in a suit in a different country deciding that."

"Makes sense."

"And we get paid more," Nicole said. "Assuming we get paid."

"You miss it?"

"No," Bridge said. "Like you said, I'm still in it, just in a different way. I'm like a baseball player who gets traded to a new team. I'm still in the game, just playing for a different organization. Mine."

"Hey, guys, heads-up," Nicole said, still monitoring the building. The others quickly took to their binoculars. "Looks like we got another car pulling up."

"Let's hope this one belongs to us."

A few seconds later, one of the car doors opened, and a woman stepped out. They couldn't yet tell if that was Dalton. Her hair was different, but in their game, hair was an easy change to make. Her back was completely to them, so they couldn't make out her face. Another door opened up, a man getting out of the passenger seat.

"Is that Kenny?" Steve asked.

Bridge focused in on the man. "That's not him."

"You sure?"

"Positive. That's not him."

The woman turned around, finally revealing her face. "That's not Dalton either," Nicole said.

Steve sighed. "Thought we had something there."

"Wonder how busy this place gets. I mean, can anyone just waltz right in here or do you need some kind of pass?"

"From what I understand, they set everything up through appointments. I think it's half-hour intervals. So if you wanna put something in, or take it out, you schedule a half-hour time period to do your business."

"Smart," Bridge said. "That way you don't have

people from different groups falling all over each other. It also means there's no mix-ups."

"And whoever's running it, their attention isn't diverted between two, three, or even four groups of people at once."

"Yeah. Whoever's running this operation knows what they're doing. How long's this place been in existence?"

"I don't know for sure. I've been here five years, and I heard about it when I first got here. And it was already well established at that point. As far as I can make out, it's been around a while. Ten, fifteen, maybe even twenty years."

"You can't operate something like this for this long without greasing a few palms with people who are high up on the pecking order."

"We know."

"Well, if people can only come in at half-hour intervals, then we got some time before the next one," Nicole said.

They waited a few more hours, with several more people coming and going.

"This place gets more action than a real bank," Bridge said.

"Almost makes you wonder, doesn't it?" Nicole replied.

"I wonder if you can deposit other things than just money in there?"

"Like what?"

"I dunno. Anything. Money, jewelry, drugs, guns, I mean, is there a limit to what you can do?"

"From what I understand, it's limited to money and jewelry," Steve said.

"Why's that?"

"Beats me. Maybe because it's smaller and easier to store?"

"I'll buy that."

After a few more people came and went, Nicole brought up the question nobody really wanted to talk about. "So how much longer are we gonna stay here?"

"Why?" Steve asked. "In a rush?"

"If Dalton and her friends were here yesterday, then yeah, I'm in a rush."

Bridge looked at the time. "We can't break it off yet. If they've already come and gone, then we're probably not gonna catch up to them, anyway. At least not for a while. But if we leave too soon, and we miss them because we got antsy, well, we're better than that."

"So we'll wait."

Bridge looked at his girlfriend and nodded. "So we'll wait. Saying a prayer might not hurt either."

"How long?" Steve asked.

"Until we're convinced that they're not showing up."

"That might take a while."

"It might. But I think we'll know. We'll get the

feeling that this is a waste of time. And I don't have it yet."

As they stared at the building for a few more minutes, another idea popped into Bridge's head. It was somewhat preposterous, even for them, but it might just work. That was, if he didn't get shot before he reached the building.

"You know what I'm thinking?" Bridge asked.

"Stop that," Nicole replied.

"What?"

"Thinking. You know it only gets us in trouble."

"Ha ha. Very funny."

"It's true."

"It's not true."

"OK." She turned to look at Steve. "It really is true."

"Stop it. OK, what if one of us goes down to that building and explains what's going on here?"

Nicole and Steve looked at each other. They each had sort of a dumbfounded look on their face. Then they turned their heads back to Bridge.

"You can't be serious," Steve said.

"Why not?"

"Because that's suicide," Nicole answered. "None of us are going to get anywhere near that building."

"Well, what if I just walk up there, say I have business, then I meet the manager and tell him what's going on?"

"Dude, you've lost your mind," Steve said. "There is no way they're going to let you in that building."

"Why not?"

Steve looked at Nicole again as if he was missing something. Nicole then took over. "Because you can't just walk in there like you know the place. They're gonna open up on you before you even get halfway there."

"Why?" Bridge said. "Doesn't seem like there's an issue pulling up."

"How do you know there's not some type of check-point that allows you to proceed somewhere up the road after we jumped off it?"

"Oh. Didn't think about that."

"And even if by some miracle they did allow you to get to the building, what do you think they're going to do to you?"

Bridge shrugged. "Let me go."

"No!" Nicole replied. "They'll kill you and dump your body."

"Not if I make a deal."

"What kind of deal could you possibly make?"

"Just that I want Dalton and company," Bridge answered. "And since I'm not a government agent, I have no interest in bringing any heat down on the building. I won't say a word about them."

"And you really think they'll buy that?"

"Why not?"

"Because they could just kill you and then be sure you'll never say a word about it."

Bridge just looked down at the grass, apparently still thinking about it.

"Are you sure you were an elite agent?" Nicole asked.

"Yeah, why?"

"Because this is dumb. You really can't be serious. I mean, you just can't be."

Bridge cleared his throat. "Uh, well, it was just an idea."

"Forget about it. OK? You're not getting into that building unless we have a couple of tanks behind us, which we don't, so just sit your ass down."

"It is down," Bridge said.

"Good. Keep it there. 'Cause if you start walking toward that building, I'll shoot you myself before they get the chance to."

Steve and Bridge looked at each other. "She wouldn't."

Bridge raised an eyebrow. "She wouldn't?"

"She would?"

Bridge gave sort of a shrug as he tilted his head. "Eh. I wouldn't put it past her."

"Oh."

"She's feisty like that."

"So I notice."

"Will you two stop jabbering like a bunch of girls and get back to business?" Nicole said.

"See?" Bridge said. "Anything happening?"

"No. I'm just tired of listening to you ladies yap in my ear."

"She prefers the action."

"I can tell," Steve said

"Yeah, and if I don't get it soon, I might accidentally shoot one of you two by mistake," she said.

Bridge rubbed his eyes and looked up at the sky. "C'mon, Dalton, hurry up and get here."

21

Six more hours passed and plenty of people came and went. Unfortunately, none of them were who Bridge was looking for. It was starting to get dark.

"We gonna wrap this up soon?" Nicole asked.

"I dunno," Bridge replied. "Does this bank close or are they open all night?"

"I believe it's guarded twenty-four hours," Steve answered.

"But can you only visit at certain times? Do they not allow anyone in after a certain point?"

Steve could only shake his head. He didn't have those answers. "I couldn't tell you."

"Keep watching and we'll find out," Nicole said.

Two more cars came and went. But finally, as darkness swept through the area, a van rolled to a stop just in front of the building.

"Who's this?" Bridge asked.

"It's not their car," Steve replied.

"How do you know they didn't change it?"

"Maybe that's the value that Kanelos brings," Nicole answered. "He's the wheelman."

"Could be."

After a minute or two, there still was no movement from the van. Nobody got out. Not even a door opened.

"What's the holdup?" Nicole asked.

Finally, after a solid minute or two, the front doors to the van opened. Bridge couldn't believe his eyes. Getting out of the passenger seat was Greg Kenny.

"That's him."

"Who?" Steve asked.

"Kenny. Passenger side."

"Well, I'll be. We did get here in time."

"That's Kanelos on the driver's side," Bridge said.

"Where's the rest?" Nicole asked.

Just as soon as the words left her lips, the back door to the van opened up. Then Zara Dalton and Chris Abbott exited the vehicle. Bridge kept his eyes focused on Abbott. He looked the same, but different. He had a hat on, but his face looked like it was changed. Not in the plastic surgery kind of way, but as if they put makeup on him. It was something. He couldn't be sure what.

"Does Chris look different to you?" Nicole asked.

"I was just thinking that," Bridge answered.

"He looks..." Then she got it and snapped her fingers. "He looks just like his brother. That's it."

"They put actor's makeup, or whatever it's called, on his face to try to alter his appearance to make him look more like his brother."

"Looks like it worked. They look almost identical."

"Yeah."

"Kind of creepy actually."

"What would they do that for?" Steve asked.

"Just like we talked about. They must've needed Gary to get money out. With him gone, they went to the next best thing: his brother."

Dalton and Abbott proceeded inside the bank, while the others waited by the van. They still didn't see Magareth, though, but they figured he must have been inside the back of the truck.

While they waited, Steve radioed down to the other members of the team who were nearby. "Team two, did you see a black van pull up here a little while ago?"

"Roger. We couldn't get a good look at who was inside, though."

"Be advised that the occupants are our targets. Repeat, the van is our target. We've got visual confirmation that four of the five occupants are definitely inside. The fifth we suspect is as well."

"What are our orders?"

"We're gonna start making our way down to your position. If the van beats us there, you start following. Keep your distance. We don't want to spook them yet. Let's let them get to their destination first, then we get them."

"Got it."

Steve started to get up, but was quickly halted by Bridge. "We should stay here until they've gone."

"What? Why? We know where they're going."

"We do?"

"Well, there's only one road out of here. They have to leave the way they came in."

"What if they don't?"

"Where else would they go?"

"Listen, in theory, you're right," Bridge said. "But what if they decide to ditch the car up the road there, then disappear into the trees on foot?"

"Why would they do that?"

"I don't know. Maybe they have another way out. Maybe they have a helicopter in a clearing patch somewhere. I don't know. But we can't just assume. We have too much riding on this."

"He's right," Nicole said. "There's a ninety-five percent chance they're gonna take that road like we figured. But if they take that other five percent, we're screwed."

"Besides, you already have a team in place down there. We don't need to be right on top of them. Sure, it'll take us a little while to get back to our car, probably putting us a good twenty, thirty minutes behind them. But we have help. Let's use it and make sure we don't make any mistakes."

Steve thought about it, looking at his two partners. He then nodded. It made sense. "Agreed. We'll wait.

We'll make sure they use that road. Guess I'm just a little anxious."

Bridge tapped him on the arm. "Happens to all of us. Your team down there. They good? Can they hold a tail?"

"Yeah. They're good."

"Good. We'll let them take the lead then. Besides, once Dalton and company are out of here, I wanna make sure they don't dump Abbott somewhere along the side of the road. 'Cause after they leave that bank, there are no guarantees anymore regarding his safety."

"Let's keep eyes on that bank to see what they bring out," Nicole said. "That's another reason for staying. If we leave early, we won't know what they have. Might be helpful for later if things go sideways."

"If?"

"When?"

It took about twenty minutes before Dalton and Abbott were seen again. They came out of the bank, each holding two black duffel bags. They took them over to the van and placed them in the cargo area.

"Four bags," Bridge said. "Looks like cash."

Dalton and Abbott then went back inside the bank again. "Must be a haul," Nicole said. "They're going back in for more."

"You didn't think they were doing this over pennies, did you?"

"Never know with some of these people."

Dalton and Abbott came out of the bank again,

once again holding a bag in each hand. They went over to the van and placed them inside. Once they were done, Abbott got inside as Dalton went over to the door to shake the hand of someone who was standing there watching.

"Must be the manager or something," Bridge said.

"Well, whoever it is, looks like they're finished," Nicole said. "They're all getting back in the car."

"Let's move!"

They quickly got up from their position and back-tracked their way to their vehicle. They moved quicker on the way back then they did on the way there, cutting a few minutes off their time. By the time they got there, they knew the van had already passed them, so they jumped in their vehicle and Steve almost put his foot through the floor.

"Team two, we're leaving our position now, have you seen the van yet?"

"Negative. Not yet."

"Keep alert, they should be coming out soon."

"We've got our eyes out."

Steve sped down the dirty road, hoping to make up some ground on the hopefully unsuspecting gang of criminals. Once they got to the end of the road, they saw the car of Team two. Steve pulled up behind them and they all got out. Steve threw his arms up in disgust.

"What are you still sitting here for?"

"They never came out!"

"What do you mean they never came out?!"

The agent shrugged, not sure how else he could explain it. "They never came out! The van never showed up."

"How can that be? There's no other road!"

"What do you want me to say? We didn't see a car come out."

Steve put his hands on his head and turned around. "Come on!"

As they continued the spirited discussion, Bridge didn't pay much attention to it. He folded his arms and put his hand near his mouth, thinking about what could have happened. Nicole came over to him and put her hand on his back.

"What is it?"

"They're still in there," Bridge replied.

"But there's no other roads, and we didn't see their van anywhere."

Bridge looked at her. "Which means there's another road. Maybe it's hidden. There's no other way. If they didn't come out, and we didn't see a car, then they have to still be in there."

Nicole nodded, agreeing. They then got Steve's attention, pulling him away from his conversation.

"Listen, if they didn't come out, they obviously still have to be in there," Bridge said. "There must be some type of side road in there that's hidden."

"Hidden?" Steve said.

"Maybe there's a bush or a tree or something lying on the side of the road to mask the entrance. It's the only explanation. Even if they ditched the car, we would have seen it. So the only logical conclusion is that they still have it. And they're using it."

"So what do you suggest?"

"We go back in there and see if we can find it. While we're doing that, see if the others can get satellite footage of this area and see if they can find a car moving." As Steve thought about it, Bridge tried to hurry up his decision. "It's the only play we got."

Knowing they had no better options, Steve quickly agreed to the plan. They all got back in their cars and started up the dirt road again. They drove slowly, getting out periodically when they found something they thought might have been a side road. While they did that, Steve had the team back at the substation looking at the satellite footage. A few minutes later, he heard back from them.

"Team one, we've got footage of a car moving west of your position."

"How far up?" Steve asked.

"About a hundred yards from your current location."

Bridge was now driving and floored it, getting to the spot in no time. They quickly got to the spot and got out of the car, looking around for the road. There was a medium-sized tree on the side of the road, lying on the ground. Bridge and Steve each grabbed one end of it and moved it further along the road.

"There it is," Nicole said. "Another dirt road."

"Just small enough to fit a car through," Steve said.

Bridge sighed and rubbed the back of his head. "Question is where's it going and how far is it gonna take to get there?"

"Only one way to find out," Nicole said. "Let's finish this thing."

22

The van finally came to a stop as it pulled up to a small cabin. It was about thirty minutes west of the bank. As the members of the gang got out of the car, a few of them weren't so sure about what they were doing there. As Kanelos started taking the bags out of the van and into the house, Kenny wanted some answers.

"What exactly's going on here? This wasn't the plan."

"This was my plan," Dalton answered. "I just never shared it with you."

"You wanna explain this?"

"Did you really think we were just gonna come out of that bank without having eyes on us? Once we got out onto that main road, there was probably a fifty-fifty chance we'd be followed. Or at least seen."

"You know that for sure?"

"No. But I'd rather take extra precautions than assume we're just smarter than everyone."

"So what's this about?"

"We're gonna wait here for a helicopter to arrive. Should be within half an hour."

"What is this place?"

"What's it look like?"

"How'd you know about it?"

"I didn't," Dalton said. "This is why Argus was needed. He knew of it. And he also knew of a chopper pilot who could get us to a place where questions wouldn't be asked. For a small fee of course."

Kenny looked at Kanelos taking the last of the bags inside. He nodded. "OK." His eyes then went to Abbott. "He's not going with us, I assume."

"We'll talk about it."

"There's nothing to talk about, Zara. You wanna say you were right about Kanelos, fine, go ahead. But there ain't no right about Abbott. He's gotta meet his brother. And now."

"And what happens if we get out of here and we find a welcoming party for us, huh? If he's gone, we have nothing left to bargain with. Nothing. You think that little bag of money is gonna stand between you and a bullet? Think again."

"You're stalling. Just do it. Do what needs to be done. If you won't, then I will. Just like last time."

Kenny walked past her, brushing Dalton in the shoulder. She turned her head to make sure he wasn't putting a bullet in Abbott's head right then and there. Kenny marched right inside, where everyone else was already, and Dalton feared what he might have been planning. She quickly went after him, getting there just in time to see him take his pistol out and point it at Abbott.

"No!" Dalton shouted, grabbing Kenny's arm. "You're not gonna do this."

"He's dead weight, Zara. We all know it except for you. Get your head out of your ass and stop dicking around." Kenny then pushed Dalton away.

Dalton wasn't gonna let the brother of the man she loved get killed right in front of her. Not if she could help it. She quickly rushed to get in front of Abbott, standing in front of him.

"If you're going to kill him, then you're going to have to kill me first."

Kenny smiled, then laughed as he put his gun down by his side. "Really? You're gonna try that trick on me? C'mon, Zara."

"I'm not letting you kill him. I let you do that once before. I'm not letting you do it again."

Kenny shrugged. "I guess you win, then." Kenny raised his arm, pointing his gun at Dalton's chest. "It's been nice working with you, but, you know, things happen. Anyway, splitting all the money two ways is a lot better than splitting it three." Dalton placed her arm behind her back, ready to pull her pistol on him. Kenny was wise to what she was doing, though. "I wouldn't do it, Zara. You'll never make it. Sorry it had to come to this."

Dalton looked at the pistol that was pointed at her. She closed her eyes as the gun fired. She flinched, expecting to feel the pain of the bullet penetrating her body. She was stunned when she felt nothing. She opened her eyes and saw blood oozing out of Kenny's chest. He then dropped to his knees, then to the ground. As he lay there, taking his last breaths, Dalton's eyes looked up, seeing Kanelos standing there, still pointing the pistol that he had just killed their partner with. He looked at Dalton and nodded.

"Whatever you say's good with me," Kanelos said. "He probably would've killed me next."

Dalton took a few steps forward and looked down at the now dead man by her feet. "Yes, Mr. Kenny, it is a shame it had to come to this. But as you said, things happen." Dalton then turned around and looked at Magareth. She wondered if he was going to have problems. He was more of a friend of Kenny's than he was with her. They kind of came along together. "Is there something you would like to say, Mr. Magareth?"

Magareth looked down at Kenny, then back at Dalton. "No."

"Do you have any issues you'd like to air?"

"I'm good."

"Great. Then we'll wait for our helicopter to arrive and get out of here together. Agreed?" Dalton looked to the others, both of whom simply nodded in agreement.

"One of you should get out there just to make sure we don't have any visitors."

"I'll go."

As Magareth left the cabin to check security, Dalton looked down at Kenny again. She supposed it would have always come down to this. Although they were still working together, it was more because they had to than because she wanted to. She never forgave him for killing Gary. And she likely never would. She had dreams about pulling the trigger on Kenny, though she wasn't sure she would ever go through with it. Now it was done.

After about twenty minutes of silence, Dalton's phone rang. It was the call she'd been waiting for.

"We're about ten minutes away from your position," a man said.

"Excellent. We'll be ready and waiting."

"How many are coming aboard?"

"Four."

"Good. See you in a few."

Dalton went outside to tell the others. She saw them walking near the trees. "We've got ten minutes before our ride arrives!"

Magareth continued walking around for a few more minutes before stopping, thinking that he heard something. It almost sounded like a car engine. It was gone now, though. He started walking down the dirt road. Then he saw it. A car. He immediately started running back to the cabin.

"We got company!"

Bridge was hidden behind a tree and jumped out, immediately firing at the running man. Magareth took cover behind the van to return fire. Steve and Nicole were only a few feet away from Bridge, and they also opened up. Within seconds, Dalton and Kanelos ran over to the van and also began firing. As both sides fired continuously, Steve shot at the van's tires, flattening a couple of them.

"There!" Steve shouted. "They aren't going anywhere now."

"Somehow I don't think that was their plan anyway," Bridge replied.

"Well, what is?"

Nicole looked up at the sky and pointed. "Probably that!"

A helicopter started circling overhead. There was a spot on the other side of the cabin that was clear enough of trees where it could land safely.

"We're gonna have to circle around if we wanna stop them from getting on that chopper," Bridge said. "You guys keep them busy."

"Is that really a choice?" Steve asked.

Bridge smiled, then went back into the woods, trying to make his way around to the other side of their opponents.

"Keep them busy!" Dalton shouted at her partners. "I'm gonna put the bags on the chopper. Then we can all get out together."

Her partners nodded, continuing to fire as their boss ran into the cabin. As the helicopter landed, Dalton came running out, trying to stay as low to the ground as possible. She had bags in each hand, as well as hanging off of each shoulder. She put them in the chopper.

"Just wait for us!" Dalton told the pilot.

The pilot looked at the activity happening nearby. "I'll give you two minutes. Then I'm gone."

Dalton ran back to the cabin to get Abbott. He stood stationary, not really wanting to move. "Come on. I promise I'll protect you, but I can't leave you here right now. You have my word."

Abbott looked at Kenny's body for a second, then walked over to her. As they went outside, they got down behind the van. Kanelos started to panic and made a beeline for the chopper.

"No!" Dalton yelled. "Wait!"

Kanelos either didn't hear her or wasn't interested in listening and kept running. By this time, Bridge had gotten to the other side of the trees, closer to the helicopter. He fired several rounds, a couple of which hit Kanelos in the upper torso. He immediately went down.

Dalton watched him go down. "Shit."

"Go," Magareth said. "I'll cover you. Then when you get to the chopper, cover me."

She looked at him and nodded. "OK." She grabbed Abbott to pull him along with her and the two of them started running for the helicopter. To get a better angle on his targets, Magareth moved out from the van. Nicole seized the opportunity and put one in the man's abdomen. He went down, but he wasn't out of the fight. He was still able to fend them off for a little bit.

Bridge stood in the same spot, ready to take Dalton out as well, but Abbott was in his line of sight. He thought he could've hit her, but there was a chance he'd miss and hit his client. He wasn't willing to take that risk, even if it was only two percent. He moved out from the cover of the trees, making himself fully visible. Upon seeing him, Dalton stopped, holding Abbot in front of her for protection.

"Don't come any closer!" Dalton yelled.

"It's over!" Bridge replied. "Give it up. You're not getting out of here."

"I don't wanna hurt anybody. Just let me get on that chopper and everything's over."

"Not everything. Just turn Abbott over. I don't wanna have to kill you."

"I've protected him! He'd be dead already if it wasn't for me."

"I kind of doubt that."

"Tell him."

"It's true, Mr. Bridge," Abbott said. "Kenny was going to kill me. She stopped him."

"Where is Kenny, anyway?" Bridge asked.

"Dead," Dalton answered. "He was going to kill Chris. I put a stop to it."

"Just turn Chris loose."

"I'll turn him loose if you give me your word you'll let me get on that chopper."

"I can't do that."

"What's it matter to you? The money's stolen from some drug cartel. It's not like I took it from a charity. Everyone should be glad it's out of their hands."

"What were you planning on doing with it?"

"All I wanna do is disappear. A new life, a new identity, a new future. Somewhere quiet on a beach where I don't have to worry about someone with a gun finding me. That's all I want. I just wanna disappear."

"Why not just turn yourself in?" Bridge asked, their guns still pointing at each other.

"I can't do that. If I'm found by that cartel, I'm as good as dead. They're already looking for me. MI6 will have me thrown in a dungeon somewhere for some of the things I've done. I've got no future looking back."

Bridge couldn't believe it, but he was actually starting to fall for her story. He was thinking about what he would do if he was in the same position. Would he have done something similar if he hadn't left the agency on good terms? He knew how hard it was to escape your past unless you erased it. As they talked, gunfire was still heard in the background, as Magareth was keeping the others at bay.

For Dalton, she knew her only hope of escaping the situation was to somehow get through to Bridge. She had to make him understand her plight.

"What would you do? If you had no other way. What would you do?"

"I don't know," Bridge answered. "But I know you've hurt some people along the way."

"I haven't hurt anyone. The only people I've hurt are the drug dealers whose pride is probably stung. That's it."

"What about Gary Abbott?"

"I loved Gary. I would never hurt him."

"Proof says otherwise."

"Kenny killed him. I didn't know. I never would've let him if I had known."

"What about the PI who came looking?"

"Kenny again. You know him, you know who he is and what he's about. You really think I could've stopped him? Everything I've done, everything, is for one purpose. And that's just to get me out of here in one piece with a new identity. I haven't killed anyone in that process. I loved Gary, I wanted him to come with me."

"You gotta let Chris go," Bridge said. "I'm not letting you take him. Even if everything you're saying is true, then you gotta prove it. Let him go. Show that you don't wanna hurt him."

"If I let him go, you're gonna kill me. Or I'll kill you. And I don't want to, Bridge. I don't want that. I just wanna get out of here."

Dalton started moving again, still using Abbott as cover as she backed her way to the helicopter. Bridge kept following. After a few more seconds, they finally made it there. She was only inches away from it.

"That's far enough," Bridge said. "You're not putting him on that chopper. Cut him loose." Bridge then decided to holster his gun. It was a risk, especially if he wasn't reading the situation right. If he was wrong, he was as good as dead. But he thought he knew what was going through Dalton's mind. "If you really meant everything you said, let him go."

Seeing that Bridge had put his gun away, Dalton took her hands off Abbott and slithered her way onto the chopper. "I'm sorry for everything I put you through." Abbott could only look at her and nod. Bridge and Dalton then locked eyes. "Everything I said was the truth, Bridge. I'm not out to hurt anyone. I just want out."

Bridge nodded and gave a half-smile. "Then I hope you get there."

The helicopter then lifted into the air as more shots were heard behind Bridge. He spun around to see Magareth dropping to the ground for the final time. Nicole and Steve then came running over to them.

"You all right?" Nicole asked.

"We're good," Bridge replied.

"What about Dalton?" Steve asked.

Bridge looked up at the sky. "Looks like she got away."

"Couldn't take a clear shot?"

"Well, she let Abbott go in return for me letting her get on there. I thought it was a trade worth taking."

Steve then went to the cabin to check inside. He came back out a minute later. "Looks like the money's gone."

"Yeah."

Bridge then had Steve take Abbott back to the car. Bridge continued staring up at the sky.

"What really happened?" Nicole asked.

"She kind of hit me in a sore spot."

"What do you mean?"

"I'll tell you about it once we get back to the hotel."

"We gonna go after her?"

Bridge shook his head. "Not me. I hope they don't either."

"Why?"

"I dunno."

"Where do you think she's going?"

"I'm not sure, but... I kinda hope she makes it."

ABOUT THE AUTHOR

Mike Ryan is a USA Today Bestselling Author. He lives in Pennsylvania with his wife, and four children. He's the author of the bestselling Silencer Series, as well as many others. Visit his website at www. mikeryanbooks.com to find out more about his books, and sign up for his newsletter. You can also interact with Mike via Facebook, and Instagram.

facebook.com/mikeryanauthor

instagram.com/mikeryanauthor